TAKEN BY STORM

by Glenna Finley

*If you hit a pony over the nose at
the outset of your acquaintance,
he may not love you, but he will
take a deep interest in your
movements ever afterwards.*
—RUDYARD KIPLING

A SIGNET BOOK
NEW AMERICAN LIBRARY
TIMES MIRROR

Copyright © 1982 by Glenna Finley

SIGNET TRADEMARK REG. U.S. PAT. OFF. AND FOREIGN COUNTRIES
REGISTERED TRADEMARK—MARCA REGISTRADA
HECHO EN CHICAGO, U.S.A.

SIGNET, SIGNET CLASSICS, MENTOR, PLUME, MERIDIAN AND NAL
BOOKS are published by The New American Library, Inc.,
1633 Broadway, New York, New York 10019

First Printing, September, 1982

1 2 3 4 5 6 7 8 9

PRINTED IN THE UNITED STATES OF AMERICA

VIRGO

"FOR ONCE IN YOUR LIFE,
DO AS YOU'RE TOLD!"

"Try and make me!" She struggled in his unrelenting grip. "Let go of me . . . you . . . you . . . beast!"

"When you learn to follow orders, I'll be glad to. In the meantime, let's see if this works." He transferred his clasp on her robe to one hand, using the other to catch her chin firmly. His mouth descended slowly and when she would have bit him, he merely tightened his hold. She gasped at his strength, relaxing her lips for one unwary instant. That was all he needed to clamp his mouth possessively over hers in a hard, urgent kiss that went on and on . . .

SIGNET Books by Glenna Finley

For Duncan

Chapter One

Only a certified, card-carrying optimist would have counted on bright sunshine on England's west coast during the last week in September. On the other hand, only the most dedicated pessimist would have forecast the torrential rain which lashed the deserted British Rail station in Truro the evening that Rosemary Lewis arrived.

She clutched the handle of her overnight bag as she finally emerged from the London express wearing her nylon raincoat, which she'd providentially brought along for a short stay in Cornwall. At the time, packing a raincoat was almost an afterthought because the London scene in early afternoon had been a gentle gray, with a few bands of blue still showing in the east. And since the weather had been that way ever since Rosemary had flown in from Seattle three days before, she hadn't given threatening forecasts more than a thought. Only the fact that she lived in the Pacific Northwest—where carrying a raincoat was automatic any time after Labor Day—influenced her choice of wardrobe.

But Seattle's mild fall weather bore no resemblance to this black, windy night where the air felt as if it came straight from the North Sea.

"Damn!" she said softly but fervently as another sheet of rain hit her shoes and stockings, forcing her to draw back under cover of the station roof. A lone streetlight reflected the shiny dark surface of a street beyond, as devoid of cars as the station was of people. Rosemary surveyed the wooden cubicle by the station door and knew that wasn't strictly true. There *had* been a platform guard huddled in that shelter when the train pulled in but he'd soon sought a warmer place to finish his shift. She shoved her hands into her coat pockets and stared angrily at the bleak pavement in front of her.

It would have been nice if she could have followed the guard's example—instead of hanging around and waiting for somebody to appear. Unfortunately, all of the taxi drivers in Truro had apparently followed the guard's example, which didn't help either.

Her mood didn't improve when she realized that the predicament was of her own making. All she'd needed to do was let events follow their natural course. In this case—the course being Simon Hardy.

Just after the train had left London's Paddington Station for the trip to Cornwall, she'd discovered him—a tall, well-dressed man in his late twenties—lingering in the aisle at her side.

"Is there something wrong?" she'd asked. "I thought I was in the right place."

"Actually you're in my seat," he'd responded apologetically, brushing his fair hair back from his forehead.

"Oh, lord—I'm sorry." She frantically searched her jacket pocket for her reservation receipt.

"No matter. I'll doss down in yours." He peered at the slip of paper tucked on top of the seat next to her. "Apparently we're both going to the same place."

"But I'm next to the window . . ."

"I've seen the view before," he said, slinging his canvas carry-all and an attaché case between the seats with accustomed ease. "And from your accent, chances are it's new to you. Be my guest."

His expression showed that a slender young woman with gleaming copperish hair and deep-blue eyes was an unexpected commuter's bonus whatever the reason. Even as he pitched his raincoat onto the rack above, he was admiring her neat profile—the small, straight nose, the firm but rounded chin, and especially the shy quirk of her smile—as she settled obediently back in her seat.

He diplomatically disappeared behind his newspaper for the early part of the trip until they left the racecourse beyond Reading. It was after Rosemary had viewed two flotillas of canal boats used to transport tourists in summer months and countless rows of neat brick houses that he put down his paper and struck up a conversation.

He introduced himself as Simon Hardy, a newcomer to the Cornwall area who'd moved south from

the Midlands a few months before. "My firm up
there went bust," he said disarmingly, "and it didn't
help that I was treasurer. Mind you, I didn't have
much to do with the collapse but who'd believe
that?"

Rosemary soothingly said that such events happened across the Atlantic, too, and it was just a good
thing that business was good in the import field at
the moment. "That's why my boss is letting me have
a chance at a buying trip over here," she added tact-
fully.

When the train reached a landscape filled with
black-and-white cows who looked as if they'd come
directly from a Constable painting, Simon suggested
they continue their discussion in the buffet.

Rosemary chose tomato soup and a piece of toast,
since she'd overlooked lunch in the flurry of
catching the train. Simon settled for steaming coffee
and a packet of plain biscuits. They carried the food
back to the comfort of their car rather than lingering
in the crowded confines of the buffet.

"So you're really coming to Cornwall on
business?" he asked when they'd reached their seats
again.

Rosemary was looking at some trailers in a bleak
hillside caravan park, but she turned back to face
him. "Why, yes. Is that so strange?"

"You just don't look like a career woman."

It was clear that he meant it as a compliment and
she smothered a smile as her attention went back to
the landscape whizzing by. A landscape, she noted

with a sudden frown, which was dimmed by the thick and sudden curtain of raindrops against the train window. Pressing her cheek against the glass, she glanced upward to see that during her journey the gray sky had darkened ominously. By then, the rain showed no signs of abating. Even the swans gliding in a lake alongside the tracks bowed their heads under the downpour. Then the impressive steeples of Exeter St. David's appeared and the weather was pushed back in her mind as Simon related the town's colorful history.

He didn't attempt anything more than superficial topics for the last hour of the journey until Rosemary reached for her raincoat when the train guard announced that the next station was Truro.

"I'd be glad to give you a lift to your hotel—if you're staying at a hotel," Simon said, pulling his mackintosh off the overhead rack and putting it on. "Sometimes the taxi service can be dicey at this time of night. Unless you've made other arrangements," he added with customary British reticence.

"Actually, I have." Rosemary didn't have to fake the regret in her tone; she was heartily wishing that she hadn't agreed to such a haywire agreement before she'd left home. "The business partner of a friend of mine is working here in Cornwall at the moment," she explained with an apologetic gesture, "and it was arranged that we should get together. He's supposed to be at the station." Even as she spoke, she wondered why on earth she was going into such detail. Probably because Simon was nice, she decided, noticing the frank disappointment on his face. It would have been fun if he'd driven her to the hotel. And after that . . .

Her wandering thoughts had come abruptly back to the present as the train slowed for the station.

"At least let me help with your heavy luggage," he said, as she retrieved a tote bag and stood up.

"I just have one. It's on the rack at the end of the car." A few passengers looked up as they passed but most stayed immersed in their newspapers, apparently bound for Penzance at the end of the line. "Do you know if the Carras Hotel is nearby?" she'd asked Simon as she caught a glimpse of the darkened, windswept station platform.

Simon had braced himself as the train ground to a halt. "About five minutes' drive. Here—allow me." The last came as he reached around her to open the door at the end of the car. He swung to the platform and put his bag down beside him before reaching up to help Rosemary with hers. "Watch the step there," he said, raising his voice over the wind and the hiss of steam from the train.

"I didn't think the place would be so deserted." She shoved the strap of her purse more securely onto her shoulder and reached down for her suitcase.

"Here, I can help you with that," Simon said as he turned back from slamming the train door.

"No, thanks—it isn't very heavy." Rosemary noticed that one of the train crew, wearing a black plastic jacket shiny with rain, had slammed the other car door, which had been left open, and disappeared.

With an eerie whistle blast, the train slowly moved off. "They don't waste any time, do they?" Rosemary asked, wondering why she'd ever left London.

"Brit Rail doing its best to live up to its advertising claims." Simon pulled the belt tighter on his raincoat and jerked his head toward the platform exit. "Your friend probably is waiting out by the street. To save you having to walk to the car park in this weather."

"Is that where your car is?"

"It had better be." Then, when she gave him an inquiring look, he went on to explain. "Sometimes my sister 'borrows' it for shopping. My brother-in-law uses theirs to go to work. Got your rail pass to show the platform guard?" he asked when she shifted her suitcase to get a firmer grip.

"I will have—in just a minute. I meant to leave it out." Rosemary put down her case again to dig in her purse. "Simon—you go ahead. It's silly for you to get even wetter."

"Well, if you're sure. Look, you'll be at the Carras for a day or two, won't you?"

"Yes, of course." Rosemary squinted in the gloom, trying to remember if she'd put the rail pass in with her passport or whether she'd left it with her traveler's checks. Under the circumstances, Simon's question only received a part of her attention—plus the fact that she was practically sure there wasn't any masculine figure waiting at the curbside beyond the station.

"Maybe we could get together for a drink tomorrow or the next day," Simon was going on. "I'll phone and set a definite time. All right?"

"I'd like that." Rosemary sounded more relieved than she intended, because she'd just discovered that she'd tucked the Rail pass into her wallet for safe-keeping. "I'll look forward to it," she added, giving Simon a brilliant smile.

As he watched, the wind blew her collar-length auburn hair back from her face, highlighting the even features and the delicate bone structure that gave her profile such classic beauty. Simon wasn't a man given to fantasies, but at that moment she could have been one of the early *Poldark* heroines, her skin damp with Cornish rain and paled by the gloom of the storm-tossed night behind her.

As he lingered unaccountably, Rosemary's expression became puzzled, then embarrassed. "Really, you don't have to worry about me," she insisted. "I'm sure that Mr. Harcourt will be along."

He continued to stare at her, but this time his fair eyebrows drew together. "Mr. Who?"

"Harcourt." She tried not to sound impatient, but the last gust of rain had trickled under her raincoat collar and Simon's tall form kept her blocked from cover. "The man who's meeting me."

"Oh, yes, of course." Simon moved at last. His smile appeared again. "I'll go along then. Try not to get too wet."

It was an effort for her not to groan at the banality of his remark, but she kept a determined smile as she nodded and watched him walk down the deserted platform and into the station. By the time she'd gotten herself organized to follow him, the platform guard had sized up the situation and done his disappearing act.

The newest occurrence increased her irritation. She'd wanted to ask if there'd been any message left for her. "So much for that," she muttered to herself as she picked up her case again and went through the darkened station ticket area.

The one streetlight that shone down on the deserted taxi rank by the curb confirmed her suspicions. Its illumination was feeble but enough to show that there wasn't any living soul awaiting her arrival.

Why in the dickens had she been such an idiot as to get involved in Gwen and Lance Fletcher's scheme at all? Because they were still in a honeymoon haze and thought togetherness was essential, they'd insisted that Lance's business partner was the only one to watch over her while she was in Cornwall. They'd been so pleasantly insistent that she hadn't dared offer more than cursory objections. Especially when Gwen had murmured mischievously that the missing Mr. Harcourt was almost as handsome as her own bridegroom. Lance had received that with a skeptical expression, merely replying that his partner was a "damned good consultant geologist," and it wouldn't hurt Rosemary to have someone making sure she ate three meals a day and didn't get blown away by the Cornish wind. There hadn't been any follow-up to the plan and suddenly it occurred to Rosemary that the elusive Mr. Harcourt might have shared her reluctance for the meeting.

But that was still no reason for him to leave her stranded, she decided irritably as she tried to stay under the station eaves while she surveyed the empty street. She pushed her case back into the archway out of the rain and squinted at her wristwatch. She'd give Lance's partner five more minutes and then she'd call a taxi from the public telephone she'd seen by the doorway. British phones terrified her with their strange rings and the split-second timing needed to insert the coins, but she'd manage to call a taxi come hell or high water.

At that moment, the wind deposited another sheet of rain on her legs and ankles and she had to smile at the aptness of her thoughts. If this kept up, she might do better trying to hire a rowboat!

She was still thinking about that when a car came around the corner and made a U-turn in front of the station. There wasn't any sign of a taxi on the doors, but her heart leapt hopefully as the driver braked to a stop at the curb and beckoned to her.

She stood, hesitating, until she recognized Simon's voice. "Come on, I'll take you to your hotel," he announced, hunching against the rain as he got out of the car. "Where's your gear?"

"By the door." Rosemary turned up her collar and waited just long enough to make sure he'd found her luggage before she made a dash for the car. She tumbled, breathless, into the passenger seat as Simon came back, slinging her things in the back.

"Don't get your bags wet," she warned him. The caution came too late; her bulky suitcase caught the edge of his attaché case on the rear seat, spilling its contents.

"Hell!" Simon spat out in exasperation, leaning over to try and straighten the mess.

"Here, let me help. This is like my hall closet," Rosemary said, trying to lever herself in position to stuff the mélange of cotton material, a handful of tools, and some tangled electrical oddments back into the leather case.

"I can manage," Simon said, brushing her aside almost brusquely. "Just sit back."

Rosemary subsided into the front seat, hoping that he wouldn't take the mishap too seriously. From the way he was scooping his belongings back into the briefcase, she'd have thought that it was gold bullion or French lingerie instead of a harmless jumble.

It was only a minute before Simon had things put to rights, and he slid back down beside her with an apologetic smile. "Now—you want to go straight to the Carras I'd wager."

"Yes, please." She turned to face him as he started the car and pulled away from the curb. "Noah must be your middle name. Do you make a habit of rescuing victims from the flood?"

"First time, actually. I didn't see your chap in the car park and it bothered me."

"It bothered me, too. I can't tell you how much I appreciate this."

"Then don't try. I'll keep you to your promise of

getting together later on. Right now, I imagine that all you want to do is have a hot cup of tea."

"Actually that's running second to the prospect of a hot bath." She was peering out the side window, trying to get an idea of the town by the buildings they were passing. "This is a lot bigger place than I imagined. Is that a cathedral I see down there?" she asked as he slowed at the top of a hill and then turned along a deserted street which wound past some impressive stone houses on either side.

"One of the biggest in the country," Simon said proudly. "You'll have to inspect it when the sun comes out again. If it ever does," he went on somewhat grimly as a gust of wind buffeted the small car.

"Do you have these storms all the time?" Rosemary asked, trying to sound matter-of-fact when actually the sight of tall trees bending under the force of the wind made her decidedly uneasy.

"Not like this. There's such a wind off the coast tonight that I understand a small freighter is in danger. The rescue units will be lucky to get the crew off in the high seas."

Rosemary grimaced, visualizing the difficulties. "Lord, I should think so. I'll keep my fingers crossed and stop complaining about my problems right now. Oh, are we here already?"

"Safe and sound," he said, pulling into the crowded parking area in front of a three-story brick building with the name "Carras" over the front door. "You'll like this place. The owners are nice people and they run a good hotel. Nothing fancy, mind you, but you'll get your money's worth. I hope you have a reservation," he added, with a sidelong, worried glance as he braked as close to the door as he could manage. "The place is usually full."

"I'm supposed to have," she added, trying not to sound concerned. Belatedly, she remembered that Daniel Harcourt was taking care of that, too. She buttoned her raincoat collar tight as she reached for the door handle. "At least the owners don't sound like the types who'd throw a tourist out in the storm. Thank you again for the lift."

"I was happy to help." He forestalled her movement to retrieve her luggage by saying, "Make a dash for it. I'll bring your things along."

When she reached the front steps of the hotel, he dropped the luggage inside and gave her a cheerful nod before hurrying back through the downpour and driving off.

Rosemary surveyed her surroundings warily and walked toward a registration counter at the back of the small foyer. There was a closed lounge door to her left and muffled sounds of conversation came from behind a closed double door marked "Bar" to the right. Just beyond the registration area there was a steep, carpeted stairway that presumably led to the hotel's guest rooms.

As Rosemary hesitated by the desk, a plump, well-corseted woman in her forties emerged from the bar area. The unmistakable sounds of partying spilled into the foyer before she could close the double doors again.

She looked surprised to see Rosemary but rallied quickly. "Have you been waiting long?"

"Just a minute or two. My name is Rosemary Lewis and I believe Daniel Harcourt made a reservation for me. He *is* staying here, isn't he?"

"Oh, yes. Mr. Harcourt always stays with us when he comes to Cornwall," the other said, looking in the reservation book. "Here you are. One single room. He didn't know how long you wanted it for and that made it difficult," she continued, giving Rosemary an apologetic glance. "There's a wedding reception this evening and most of the guests are staying over with us. Oh, heavens—now what?" The last followed the sound of breaking glass from behind the double doors. The manageress made a beeline for the bar, saying over her shoulder, "I'll send my husband back to show you your room in just a minute, Miss Lewis."

"That's all right. Don't worry about . . ." Rosemary broke off in mid-sentence as the other disappeared behind the quickly closed door. After waiting for five minutes in splendid solitude, she decided she could either join the wedding party or find her room for herself.

The latter suggestion was infinitely more appealing and she pulled the registration book around to see that room 3 was pencilled in between Daniel Harcourt's name and her own. Probably because he'd made the reservation, she decided, and took a key marked with number 3 from a pigeonhole arrangement behind the counter. Then she picked up her bag and made her way up the stairs.

The upper hallway was a mixture of Victorian castoffs, with a worn carpet runner and a faded rose print on the chair next to some pot plants in bamboo containers. The wood floor was polished and bright, however, and there was a reassuring smell of disinfectant when Rosemary passed a public bathroom. Its immaculate condition didn't prevent her from hoping there was a private bath connected with room 3, which she'd just discovered on her left. After unlocking the door, she gave a sigh of relief as she saw the room was unoccupied and there was an unwrinkled spread on the double bed.

By then, she felt as if she'd left London days rather than hours before, and she couldn't wait to get out of her damp clothes. She closed the door behind her and left her bag atop a bulbous oak dresser, even as she noted a mammoth wooden armoire which apparently served as the room's closet. An open door beside it revealed the hoped-for private bathroom. She inspected the old-fashioned tub with approval as she shrugged out of her nylon raincoat and hung it from a hook on the back of the door to dry. Then she turned on the taps to fill the tub. After a warm bath, there'd be time to go down and see somebody about a dinner reservation. Even if the place were crowded with wedding guests, they couldn't expect her to venture out in the storm again. And while she was discussing dinner, she'd ask if Daniel Harcourt had ever appeared to claim *his* hotel reservation.

Not that she particularly cared, since she now had a roof over her head and bathwater running in the next room. When she did encounter the man, she'd simply accept his apology and let him go on his way. She'd have to remember to thank him for putting her in this hotel, she decided, as her glance swept swiftly over the old-fashioned, high-ceilinged room. The decor might give an interior designer fits, but it was comfortable and almost warm. She'd found the last two words applied to most hotels in England—whether they were the luxury variety or not. Fortunately, she'd packed with that in mind and included wool slacks as well as sweaters and skirts. She'd left most of them in her other suitcase, which was stored in London, but there was a pleated tartan skirt and turtleneck sweater available for dinner downstairs. It was a cheerful outfit as well as being the warmest thing in her suitcase.

She let the water fill the tub, pouring in herbal bubble bath as a final luxury, and stayed in its perfumed depths until the water temperature finally cooled. Then she emerged and hastily reached for the biggest towel on the rack. She'd just started to dry herself when footsteps from the outer hall made her freeze on the bathmat. A sudden draft under the bathroom door at that moment made her realize that *freeze* was certainly the operative word; she'd do exactly that unless she dried herself in double-quick time and got some clothes on.

Another sound, appreciably closer, made her pause

again just as she was dropping the towel over the rack. She frowned, trying to visualize what was happening outside; surely the door to her room couldn't have come ajar when someone went down the corridor. Not hesitating any longer, she snatched up the thigh-length nylon robe which she'd brought as a makeshift dressing gown. She wrapped it around herself, muttering in annoyance as it clung to her damp skin even as she pulled open the bathroom door with her other hand.

Almost convinced that she was imagining things, she'd taken two steps into the bedroom before realizing that the man standing just inside the door was truly flesh and blood.

At any other time, the possibility of overlooking such a considerable specimen of masculinity would have been ridiculous. He was at least six feet tall, with shoulders that looked almost that wide in a yellow rain jacket still damp from the storm. His hair had been plastered by that same rain so that it resembled a thick, dark cap just reaching the collar of a blue chambray work shirt which matched his worn pair of jeans. A wide leather belt with a battery hanging from it completed his outfit. There was no doubt that such down-to-earth clothes fitted him; he emanated an aura of whipcord strength even as he stood there looking her over, his eyebrows in an ominous line and his gray eyes as bleak as the weather outside. His voice, when it came, was deep and just as implacable as his manner. "I don't know what

you think you're playing at, young lady, but I'm
sure as hell not in the mood for games tonight." He
reached a careless hand toward her open suitcase and
tossed her the sweater and skirt she'd left on top.
"Put these on and beat it."

Rosemary was so incensed by that hateful "young
lady" sarcasm that she reacted instinctively. The
sweater and skirt were sent flying back in his face.
"Who do you think you're ordering around? Get out
of my room this minute or I'll scream for the manager."

As his jaw hardened and he took a warning step
toward her, she suddenly realized that she wasn't in
any position to wage war with a man who topped
her by ten inches and almost as many years. There
was no doubt he was in his early thirties—his kind of
assurance didn't come without experience. All kinds
of experience, she discovered, watching his gaze do a
deliberate intinerary from the top of her head down
to her toes. He didn't miss an inch of the revealing
territory on the way, as her wrap was still clinging
to her damp curves.

Then, suddenly, his gaze came back up to hers, and
his frown deepened as he snapped, "What do you
mean? Your room? Who in the devil are you?"

"Rosemary Lewis," she flared back, "although I
don't know what business . . ." She broke off as his
heartfelt groan seemed to bounce off the walls.
"What's the matter? What have I said now to . . ."
Her own voice dropped. "You're Mr. Harcourt?"

There was no doubt that she wanted him to deny it. He watched her take a nervous step backward and gave a cursory nod, showing he wasn't enchanted by the situation either. "Dan Harcourt. I'm sorry there's been a mixup," he went on without any perceptible remorse. She stared at him wide-eyed as he bent to pick up the skirt and sweater from the carpet in front of his steel-toed work boots. This time, he handed her clothes back to her. The gesture was more polite, perhaps, but just as definite nonetheless. "We can straighten it out down at dinner. Right now, I'd like to get changed, so if you don't mind . . ."

Rosemary galvanized into action before he could close the bathroom door as he walked past her. "Just a darned minute! You can't do this. I don't care if you are Lance's partner—I didn't agree to anything about sharing a room."

He lingered in the doorway, his mouth stern. "My feeling exactly, Miss Lewis. Only this happens to be *my* room. I dropped my suitcase off this morning before I went to work and if you'd bothered to look in there," he gestured toward the armoire, "you'd see most of my wardrobe. Mrs. Carras will show you your room when you get back down to the desk. And when you're there, better make us a reservation for dinner. I have no objections to sharing a table with you."

He was in the bathroom with the door firmly closed and locked behind him before Rosemary could reply. She did manage to kick the bottom of the wooden panel as hard as she could before she remembered that she wasn't wearing any shoes. There was no doubt he heard her gasp of outrage and pain because she clearly heard his smothered laughter just before he turned on the water in the tub.

Chapter Two

If Rosemary had hoped for sympathy from the hotel's owners, she found quickly that she was destined for disappointment there, too.

She arrived back at the reception counter still breathing hard from throwing her clothes on and getting out of room 3 before that accursed bathroom door opened again. Her suitcase was a jumbled mess and she knew that her hair looked almost worse than when she'd come in from the storm—the one that still raged outside.

"You don't mean that you were in Mr. Harcourt's room?" the plump manageress had asked, scandalized, as soon as she'd answered Rosemary's firm finger on the counter bell and heard her abbreviated explanation. "Don't tell me that my husband didn't check the list." She pulled out a typewritten copy from under the ledger and showed it to Rosemary. "It says right here that you're to be in room 25. I'm sorry that it's in the annex but I had to move some other guests around to accommodate you at all. If Mr. Harcourt hadn't been so anxious to have you enjoy your first visit to Cornwall, I wouldn't have taken your reservation. By the way, is he coming down to dinner?"

"Yes." Rosemary chewed uneasily on the edge of her lower lip. "I was supposed to tell you to save a place."

"For the two of you, I hope?" Mrs. Carras was writing busily on still another list. "Otherwise, it will be quite a wait for single tables."

"How long?" Rosemary asked, thinking that even starvation would be preferable to facing the overbearing Mr. Harcourt across a tablecloth and having to be civil when she'd like to dump the soup in his lap.

"An hour at least," Mrs. Carras said, consulting her list. "Maybe more. Miss Dove eats so slowly."

"And if Mr. Harcourt and I share a table?"

"I can take care of you right away. He won't be long coming down, will he?"

Rosemary shook her head, knowing she'd lost again. Principles were all very well but at that moment the tempting dining room odors wafting through the front hall were too much for her to overcome. "I can go on in and start if that will help. I know how busy you are."

The plump manageress's face took on a look of concern. "But you haven't even been to your room."

"It doesn't matter." Rosemary had no intention of confessing that she'd already sampled the amenities of number 3. "Could I just leave my bag over there against the wall and take it with me later?"

"There's no need for that. I'll have my husband carry it down as soon as he has a minute." Mrs. Carras handed over a brass key with a heavy disc which said 25.

"If he's so busy, he doesn't have to bother. I can manage."

"Actually, you have to go up one flight of stairs and then down two others at the back for the annex. It's a bit complicated," Mrs. Carras said, her eyes not quite meeting Rosemary's. "I'm sorry that we don't have anything better."

"I'm sure it will be just fine," Rosemary assured her, although she knew in her bones that room 25 was going to be a far cry from what she'd hoped. "Shall I go on into the dining room then?"

"Of course, dear." The other woman sounded glad to get back on safer ground. "Just follow me. There's a nice table by the window that Mr. Harcourt seems to like."

From her hushed tone, Daniel Harcourt might have been visiting royalty. Rosemary gritted her teeth, knowing better than to ask why he was in a prize room on the second floor and she was relegated to a broom closet in the annex. It was just because she was hungry and tired that she felt spiteful, she told herself as they went into a crowded dining room with windows along one side.

Mrs. Carras seated her at the only vacant table and said that she'd have a waitress with her directly. Rosemary was left staring at a menu and a starched white tablecloth, which was preferable to her glimpse of the storm-tossed night visible through the curtains. Despite her turtleneck sweater, Rosemary shivered as she waited for someone to take her order.

"Will you be wanting to wait for Mr. Harcourt, miss?" It was a pretty young blonde dressed in a peasant blouse and gathered skirt who hovered by the table en route to the kitchen. "I could bring you a glass of wine, if you'd like."

"I'd rather order dinner, thanks. Could I have some coffee first of all? To try and get warm."

The girl shook her head firmly. "Coffee's served in the lounge. After the meal," she added so that there could be no misunderstanding.

"Then I'll just go ahead and order dinner," Rosemary said, undaunted. "The soup, please, and roast beef later. And, if it's not too much trouble, a glass of water."

"Of course, miss."

Rosemary felt a flicker of triumph, which faded abruptly as the waitress smiled and said, "Oh, Mr. Harcourt—Mrs. Carras said you'd be in. Shocking night, isn't it?"

The geology consultant, now dressed in a well-tailored gray Harris tweed sport coat and flannel slacks, lowered himself into a chair across the table and smiled at the young waitress. "Rotten, but I couldn't stay away. Not with roast beef on the menu."

"Soup or fruit cup?"

"Soup, I guess. And we'll have that red wine your boss is touting."

The girl bestowed a dubious look on Rosemary, as

if suddenly recalling her presence. Then her glance went back to Daniel. "Two glasses of wine?"

"Of course."

He was so definite that she nodded and moved off even as Rosemary started to protest. "I'd already said that I didn't want any wine, Mr. Harcourt."

"So you've changed your mind." He indicated the plate of rolls in the middle of the table and helped himself when she shook her head.

The waitress was back with a carafe of red wine and two glasses before Rosemary could think of a possible subject which would show him that she was only there under sufferance. It didn't help that she focused on one insignificant fact. "She forgot my water," Rosemary said with outrage and then felt like a fool when his eyebrows lifted reprovingly.

To his credit, he didn't say anything. He simply looked around and got up to take a pitcher of water and an empty glass from a serving cart not far away. He poured her water and sat down again, leaving the pitcher at her elbow.

"Thank you," she acknowledged, sounding less than charming.

"You're welcome," he replied, copying her aloof air. Then he slapped his palm down on the table so abruptly that the carafe bounced. "Oh, for God's sake, come off it!"

Rosemary's mouth fell open in amazement and she glanced around, hoping that he hadn't attracted the attention of the entire room. Surprisingly, none of the other diners seemed to have paid any attention to his outburst. Nevertheless, her expression was severe as she turned back. "You have an almighty nerve complaining about *my* behavior. What's your angle? A 'begin as you mean to go on' party?"

"Don't be ridiculous." He reached for the carafe of wine and filled their glasses. "Lance didn't tell me that you sulked."

"I don't. I mean—I scarcely know your partner. I've known his wife for a long time, though. She didn't tell me that you threw women out of hotel rooms with such abandon either."

As soon as the words passed her lips, she knew that she'd made a mistake. Even before he mimicked with deadly accuracy, "I don't. I mean—I've scarcely met Lance's wife so how could she know about all the skeletons in my closet?"

"I don't think that's funny at all. You made me feel—like a trollop. Pretending that I was trying to take advantage of you."

His hand went up to rub his chin, but not fast enough to cover his grin. "Is *that* the impression I gave? I'll be honest with you—I didn't feel threatened at all. If I hadn't had a lousy day, I might have let you stay." He took a sip of wine. "At least for a little while."

Rosemary felt the blood surge up her cheeks. Glaring at him she said, "At least I can be grateful for small favors. Let me tell you, friend, you've either been reading the wrong books or flirting with the wrong women." She added the last when the waitress served their soup and left again after a limpid smile in his direction. "Like that one. She's a little young for you, isn't she?"

"I'll remember your advice if I'm ever tempted to ask her out." He picked up his soup spoon carefully. "I'm sorry that we don't have more time to trade insults, Miss Lewis, but I promised Lance that I'd look out for you and that's the way it's going to be. I'll make it as painless as possible for both of us."

She relaxed and picked up her own soup spoon, relieved at that first suggestion of an olive branch. "Just so you understand that this 'big brother' act wasn't my idea."

"Oh, you've convinced me of that by now. You will admit that your appearance was misleading."

"It wouldn't have happened if it hadn't been for that wedding reception," she muttered, her eyes determinedly on her food. "Or if the people who run this place would keep decent records."

"You've lost me . . ."

"I'm just saying that the number 3 in their book was between our names and nobody told me it was your room. It certainly didn't look occupied. You couldn't have spent much time there," she added defensively.

"I just had a few minutes to drop off my things before I went down to the mine this morning. It didn't occur to me to leave a paper trail of socks and shirts to the bathroom."

"Very funny."

"No, it wasn't." He put his spoon down on the plate alongside his empty soup dish and then put up a hand to rub his neck wearily. "You're right about my manners—they seem to have gone out the window. Maybe it's this damned weather."

His apology sounded sincere and it caught Rosemary by surprise. She stared across the table at him, noting that the stern lines at the corners of his mouth were pronounced and that his gray eyes were shadowed with weariness. Her own glance narrowed as she asked, "Exactly what happened down in that mine today?"

His glance shot up to hold hers. "What do you know about that?"

"Look," she gestured helplessly, putting her soup spoon down at the last minute and shoving her dish away. "I'm so dense that I don't even know what kind of a mine we're talking about. All I know is that you and Lance are consultant geologists and that you sound like somebody at the end of his tether. At first, I thought I was responsible." She smiled and thought there was a flicker of response, but it was so fleeting that she decided she must have imagined it. "I don't think I could drive you to drink all by myself."

The corners of that stern mouth quirked and he took another sip from his glass. "One carafe of wine. And it's tin. The mine," he added as she stared, uncomprehending. "You were right about the rest, too. It was a hell of a day. When you come in on the heels of a mine explosion it's apt to be that way."

"Good Lord, was anybody hurt?"

"Three men were hospitalized with smoke inhalation. They were near asphyxiation and unconscious when the rescue team got to them but they'll be okay. Actually, everybody else was lucky. The thing blew at a shift change or there would have been lots more victims."

Rosemary shook her head somberly. "Somebody must be watching over them."

"I'm beginning to think so. It's the second explosion this month. Both during the shift change. That's either an almighty coincidence or something that doesn't have anything to do with luck."

Her eyes widened. "You mean it could have been deliberate?"

"I've been retained to pursue all the possibilities." He stopped speaking long enough to let the waitress put down their orders of roast beef and nod when she asked if they'd like mustard. "Give it a try," he told Rosemary when she would have turned it down. "It's better than the horseradish," he said when they were alone again, "and sometimes their Yorkshire pudding needs help."

"It looks delicious to me," Rosemary said, picking up her fork. "Lunch on the train was a little thin and a long time ago." Her first bite of the entrée revealed that it was tender but bland. She tried mustard on the second and discovered that Daniel was right. In this case it didn't matter, but she hoped that it wasn't setting a precedent. Without even trying, he made her feel as unnerved as the time she'd attended a reception and carried on a fifteen-minute conversation with the guest of honor while struggling to detach her fork from the center of a sticky meringue and balance her coffee cup at the same time.

She cut another bite of roast beef with care and tried to keep just the right amount of cool interest in her voice. "This mine where you're working—is it nearby?"

"Wheal Tamar? Not far."

"What did you call it?"

"Wheal Tamar." His tone was impatient until he saw that she was honestly puzzled. "Sorry, I forgot that you'd just arrived. *Wheal* is the Cornish word for mine. There've been all sorts of Wheal Marys, Wheal Margarets, Wheal Kittys over the years here. The name Tamar in this case was taken from the river of that name."

"It sounds like something out of a Gothic novel. And this storm," she nodded beyond the window, "fits right in."

"Unfortunately for the people at Wheal Tamar it's damned real. And it could be the final straw. They were having problems keeping the company solvent before this last trouble."

"That's another reason they called you in?"

"Ummm." His lips firmed in that stern line she was beginning to recognize. He jabbed at his last bite of Yorkshire pudding and then obviously decided it wasn't worth the trouble. Putting his knife and fork at the edge of his plate, he leaned back and fixed his glance on hers. "I don't know why I'm monopolizing the conversation. What are you doing in this part of the world? Lance mentioned that it was in connection with your job. What do you do for a living?"

"I'm with an import-export company. Our head office is in Seattle, so we usually concentrate on Pacific Rim countries for our buying sources."

"But now Cornwall?" His eyebrows had drawn together at her words. "You've got me wondering. Other than mining and fishing and holiday resorts, what is there here?"

Her expression was more demure than she felt. "Would you believe dolls?"

He nodded slowly. "Their new cottage industry. It seems to me I saw something about that on the BBC a week or so ago."

"My boss heard about it last month, and since I was planning to be in London he thought I would like an expense-paid detour."

"I take it that you didn't need much persuading . . ."

"For an extra week in England?" Her smile had a touch of gamine. "He didn't know it, but I would have paid him."

"So how did Lance and his bride get into it?"

"I had dinner with them the night I'd gotten the green light. You know how newlyweds can be, or do you?" She glanced at him curiously. "Maybe bachelors aren't considered fair game these days."

"Let's just say that Lance hasn't asked me to watch over any redheads lately."

"I'm not a redhead. Not really." She put up a hand to brush a thick strand back from her cheek automatically. "It's more brown than red and right now it's a mess. The rain at the station didn't help."

"I'm sorry about that, too. It took me longer to get back to Truro than I'd figured." He looked around, as if impatient with the steamy dining room and the rising hum of conversation from the other guests. "Look—do you want dessert?"

"Well, I guess not." It wasn't strictly true because the roast beef hadn't really made up for her sparse lunch, but there wasn't any way she could admit it without sounding like a Sumi wrestler.

"Then let's get out of here. The humidity makes it feel like the inside of an oyster and I've had enough of being closed in." He got up and shoved his chair back, waiting for her to come around the table before gesturing her ahead of him. "This way, we can beat the crowd to the lounge."

"Oh, yes, the coffee." A wry note crept into Rosemary's tone.

He gave her a sideways grin as they made their way out of the dining room. "The only way to beat the system is to stay in a tourist hotel while you're in London. Here in Cornwall—it's served after dinner in the lounge."

"When it's too late and you're out of the mood."

"Exactly." He paused by a warming tray with a glass jug of coffee atop it surrounded by demitasse. "Black or white?"

"White, I guess." She looked around the deserted room, where three vinyl-covered couches cozied up to an inadequate electric heater. "You were right about beating the crowd."

He nodded and deposited her cup on the end table closest to the heater. "I'd offer to take you out to some place more festive but tonight I think we'd be blown off the block."

"That's what Simon said. Apparently there's even a freighter in trouble off the coast."

He frowned as he settled on the couch beside her. "Who's Simon?"

"Simon Hardy—a man I met on the train. After you stood me up, he rescued me at the station and brought me to the hotel. He's even offered to take me around while I'm here," she added, aware that she was embroidering the truth but deciding it was in a good cause.

Daniel's frown didn't disappear. "What does he do?"

Her poise took a momentary nosedive. "I didn't ask him. He came from the Midlands and said something about being the treasurer in a firm there." There was no point in mentioning his company's bankruptcy, she told herself. All she wanted was to show Daniel Harcourt that he didn't need to worry about her. If he thought there was somebody more than willing to take over, that didn't hurt anything either. He deserved a setdown after the way he'd acted. She took an absent-minded swallow of coffee and almost choked on the lukewarm, bitter brew. "I should have had dessert," she said, forgetting to be diplomatic.

"Hell, why didn't you say so? We can go back in."

"No—of course not. Pay no attention." She gamely took another sip of coffee before putting her cup on the end table. "I'd better go and find my room."

"It's still pretty early," he said, looking at his watch.

Rosemary knew exactly what time it was but she was also remembering that she'd stowed a chocolate bar in her suitcase before leaving London. She managed a yawn and got to her feet. "I know, but I have a big day tomorrow. If I can get in touch with Mrs. Rome in the morning, I can check their production output. It's one thing to be sure they have a good product but . . ." She broke off as he snapped his fingers. "What is it?"

"Rome." He stood up beside her and left his own coffee on the nearby plaster mantel. "What's her husband's name?"

"I haven't the foggiest. Why?"

"It isn't a very common name in this part of the world. I was just struck by the coincidence."

Some coincidence, Rosemary thought. He'd taken the bait like a hungry barracuda. "If you really want to know, I'll ask her tomorrow. There can't be more than one Claire Rome who makes rag dolls in Truro. I'll leave a note for you at the desk."

"That isn't necessary. I imagine we'll run into each other before long." As he shoved his hand in his coat pocket, his expression changed noticeably. An instant later, she saw the reason for it as he pulled out a familiar travel toothbrush case from his pocket. "You left this behind tonight. At least, I presume it's yours."

Just because she'd taken a fancy to a case that had a small bear cub on the end was no reason for him to act as if she were a perennial Peter Pan, Rosemary thought angrily. She retrieved the offending case and said, "I hope I didn't leave anything else. There wasn't a chance for me to search the premises without giving you some other wrong ideas."

He made no effort to hide the amusement in his glance. "That certainly would have given me ideas."

"Not that you needed any help on that score."

There was no telling how he might have responded if Mrs. Carras hadn't stuck her head into the lounge at that moment, saying with relief, "Oh, Mr. Harcourt—I wasn't sure where you'd gone. There's a lady on the telephone for you. You can take it at the desk."

"I'll go on to my room," Rosemary announced, starting for the door before Daniel could reply. "I'll probably see you tomorrow."

"You can be sure of that," he said in a low voice that nevertheless carried clearly to her ears before she could escape.

When Rosemary reached her room in the annex a few minutes later after a complicated up-and-down route through dimly lit hallways, she took one look at the cramped quarters and felt an irresistible urge to dash back to Daniel's room and establish squatter's rights before he got off the phone.

A second glance left her shaking her head as she went in and closed the door, finally sitting down on the single bed, which took up fully half the room. Crowded on the other side was a vinyl-covered chair with some upholstery strapping hanging from the bottom of it and a small table topped with a minuscule lamp. Above the bed, a shelf contained a Bible and a speaker box with a single switch marked "Office." She turned and looked back to the door, noticing for the first time that a shower curtain on one side hid a lavatory, while a row of hooks on the opposite wall served for a closet.

Moving to the window at the far wall, she pushed aside two strips of pink cretonne to peer out onto a car hood just three feet away. Apparently she was within spitting distance of the parking lot. It would be handy if she owned a car or planned on skipping out without paying her bill, she decided, but it was a dead loss as a postcard view. Not that she was tempted to hang around the window—even as she stood there, drafts from the stormy gusts outside seeped around the edges of the frame. She pulled the cretonne back into place and turned to hoist her suitcase onto the table.

Pulling out a hot water bottle, which she'd providentially packed along with a flannel nightgown, she moved over to check the temperature of the water in the basin. Steam gushed out of the hot faucet almost immediately and a smile came over her face for the first time since she'd entered the room. At least she'd be warm when she got into bed, and that was enough to cancel out almost all the other drawbacks.

And there was one other asset, she remembered suddenly. Reaching into her suitcase, she unearthed the candy bar which was going to take the place of dessert, midnight snack, and all the rest.

Tomorrow, she'd have to see about replenishing her supply of calories. All she had to do was detour by a grocery store on her way to meet Claire Rome.

For with Daniel Harcourt watching over her from his perch on the second floor, it was a foregone conclusion she'd need all the strength she could muster.

Chapter Three

The rattle of crockery in the hallway outside her door awakened Rosemary hours later. As she squinted across the room, trying to read the dial on her travel alarm, she noted the absence of rain against the windowpane and decided that at least the storm had passed. Then she heard another discreet tapping and realized what was going on—it was the disconcerting British custom of early morning tea.

She almost groaned aloud, wondering why she hadn't thought to tell the management that she didn't want any. Hearing a knock at the room next door and the murmur of a feminine voice, she knew it was too late to stop delivery. She pushed back the covers and got to her feet just as a rapping sounded on her own door. "I'm coming," she called, reaching for her robe at the end of the bed and knocking her cold hot water bottle onto the floor in the process. "Damnation!" she muttered, trying to sort things out as another determined rap came from the hallway. "Hold on—I'll be right there," she responded. She shrugged into her robe with difficulty as she was still clutching the hot water bottle, and made her way to the door. Nothing happened when she turned the knob because she'd carefully locked herself in the night before. "Oh, for pete's sake," she murmured, tucking the hot water bottle under one arm as she fumbled with the key. All this for a cup of tea that she wasn't going to drink!

When she finally got the door open, she started to say, "You needn't have bothered," to the woman she expected to find in the hallway and finished with, "Good Lord, what are *you* doing here?" when she saw Daniel there instead, with a cup of tea. He was immaculately dressed in another sport coat and flannels and looked as if he'd been up for hours. Apparently it was *her* cup of tea he was holding, because he didn't waste any time marching in and putting it beside her open suitcase. "I'm just saving some time," he responded, "so I told the girl that I'd bring yours in."

"I didn't think that you were working the early morning shift in the annex," she said, staying by the door. "Aren't you going overboard on this chaperoning bit?"

"Drink your tea before it gets any colder." As he looked around her crowded quarters, a grim expression settled over his features. "I didn't know you were going to be stuck in anything like this."

His candid confession made everything tolerable suddenly. Rosemary deposited her hot water bottle in the basin and closed the hall door. "It looks worse than it really is. There's plenty of hot water and the mattress wasn't bad." She took a sip from the cup he'd brought and wrinkled her nose.

"I feel the same way about lukewarm tea first thing in the morning," he said, retrieving the cup and walking over to pour the remainder down the drain. "Now—you're in the clear."

"And if anybody asks—I'll tell them it was delicious." She saw him surveying the candy bar wrapper in the wastebasket with amusement. "Is there anything else you want to know?" she asked without attempting to hide her sarcasm.

He didn't bother to reply. Instead, he put a hand on the chair cushion to test it and then turned to perch on a corner of the table.

Rosemary admired his decision, because the chair wouldn't have supported a well-nourished midget. "Are you always so cautious?"

"Most of the time. I'm an expert on stress factors. That's part of my job," he said drily. "You'd better get back under the covers. Even that flannel nightgown won't keep you from freezing in here."

"I'd planned on getting dressed."

"I won't keep you long."

At that moment, he looked as immovable as the Sphinx, and equally austere. Rosemary knew she'd be foolish to protest, so she marched back to the bed and got under the thin coverlet, bracing herself against the wall.

Daniel gave a nod of satisfaction and folded his arms over his chest. "I have to be at the mine for most of the morning but I should be finished by noon. After that, I'll be able to chauffeur you around for the rest of the day. There's no need for you to try and do it by taxi."

She stiffened in protest. "I wouldn't think of bothering you. If it isn't convenient to get a taxi, there certainly must be a car-hire place in a town this size. Besides, I really think that Simon will be in touch."

"Well, until he comes out of the bush, you'd better settle for a bird in the hand. If you see your Mrs. Rome this morning, we can spend the afternoon sightseeing. I imagine you'd enjoy Tintagel."

"King Arthur's castle?" she asked, momentarily diverted. "Oh, I'd love to see it. But there really isn't any need for you to go to the trouble."

"I told Lance that I'd watch out for you." He moved to the door and opened it. "You can leave word at the desk after breakfast when you know about your appointment with the doll lady. At any rate, I'll see you here at lunch time. And don't worry about this room," he added, lingering on the threshold. "I'll talk to Mrs. Carras and arrange something better for you tonight. In the meantime, you'd better take a hot shower. You're beginning to turn blue." He disappeared into the hallway, closing the door firmly behind him.

Rosemary clamped her lips together, vowing she'd ask if there were a stray bulldozer in his ancestry the next time she saw him. Which would *not* be at lunch if she had anything to do with it.

She shivered as she got out of bed and went over to

check the mirror above the basin. Her skin wasn't blue, she decided, inspecting it in the pale light cast by the ceiling bulb. If anything, it looked gray. Just like her flannel nightgown, which had been a pleasant pale blue when she'd bought it in London. No wonder Daniel had suggested that she get into bed and cover up.

She shivered again and decided to follow his advice about the hot shower. And after some reviving coffee at breakfast, she'd take her problems one by one.

A half-hour later in the dining room, she found that the coffee was just as she liked it. So were the scrambled eggs and Danish bacon. That made up for the burnt offerings of toast which cooled in the chrome toast rack at her elbow.

There weren't many tables occupied in the room. Either the wedding guests were still in their beds or had breakfasted earlier as she suspected Daniel had.

Mrs. Carras confirmed her suspicion when she came into the room, like a galleon under sail. She paused by Rosemary's table with a worried look. "Mr. Harcourt asked if we could change your room when he came in for coffee. I told him that you'd been told it wasn't up to our usual standard."

"Mr. Harcourt just hoped that there might be a more spacious room available," Rosemary said. "It doesn't have to be as big as his."

"There aren't any others as big as his," Mrs. Carras said, setting her straight on that score. "It's the best in the house. But there is a small room next door to his that's now available. We usually offer the two of them as a family suite. You'll share the bath with Mr. Harcourt." She met Rosemary's startled gaze blandly. "He said that would be satisfactory."

Anything was better than being stuck in the annex, Rosemary decided, thinking fast. "Yes, of course."

"Naturally, we wouldn't have suggested it if you weren't friends."

The wealth of British understatement in her voice made Rosemary blush furiously. "Naturally. When do I move?"

"There's no need to hurry," Mrs. Carras said, reverting to the gracious innkeeper. "Mr. Harcourt's already gone out. That same woman was on the phone to him again this morning." Then, as if regretting her indiscretion, she hurriedly said, "Do finish your breakfast. Can I get you some fresh hot toast?"

"Thanks, I'd love some. To go with another cup of coffee, if you wouldn't mind."

When Rosemary finally was directed back up the front stairway—this time to room 2, she found her bag already inside and her raincoat folded on top of it. The room was about a third the size of Daniel's next door, but it was freshly painted in pale pink and a new satin spread was atop the single bed pushed against one wall. There was a small portable wardrobe just large enough for Rosemary to put her suitcase out of sight at the bottom. Other amenities included a tiny radio on the bed table and a view over some Georgian houses toward the center of town.

She peered around the connecting door to the bathroom and afterward carefully turned the key on her side. Later, she and Daniel could work out a system to avoid bumping into each other.

She gave a sigh of satisfaction as she went back into the bedroom and walked over to the window. How silly she'd been to have any misgivings about the arrangement! Just as if two intelligent adults couldn't share one bathroom without turning things into a French farce.

A feeling of satisfaction settled over her. She'd come through all the pitfalls and now things were finally working the way they were supposed to. Even the weather seemed an indication of it. The storm had blown itself out, leaving the sky a beautiful clear blue with puffy white clouds that must have arrived from the Mediterranean. There was even sunshine, albeit British sunshine, with a pale, "trying hard" look, but cheerful nonetheless. Rosemary stared down the hillside to the street beyond and saw schoolboys in neat gray-and-blue uniforms headed toward a big stone building, fronted by a magnificent wrought-iron fence. They weren't hurrying, taking time to laugh and scuffle as if enjoying the freedom and sunshine, too. The distinctive spires of Truro's cathedral towered over other buildings in what appeared to be the center of town. Rosemary decided she'd have to put that on her schedule of sightseeing and made mental apologies to the city fathers for thinking that Truro was merely a wide spot in the road.

She said as much on the postcard that she wrote to Lance and Gwen Fletcher—with a casual postcript that she and Daniel had met. The latter came after she'd almost written "gotten together" and hastily changed the wording.

Going downstairs a little later, she asked Mrs. Carras about mailing her card and the location of a public telephone. She was told that the postbox was down the next block in the middle of a gate—"you can't miss it"—and she was welcome to use the hotel phone on the desk. "We'll just add the charge to your account."

Rosemary found that there was only one Rome listed in Truro, with a home address of Alexandra Drive. She crossed her fingers as she put through her call, letting the phone at the other end ring a long time, and was about to hang up when a faint feminine voice finally answered.

"Mrs. Rome?" Rosemary asked cautiously, wondering if she'd gotten the wrong number after all. The woman at the other end sounded as if she hardly had enough energy to say "hello" let alone run a thriving cottage industry. "I'm Rosemary Lewis—from Global Imports in the States. I wrote to you about the dolls you're making."

There was a sharp, indrawn breath at the other end of the wire and what sounded suspiciously like a muffled groan.

"I *do* have the right Mrs. Rome, don't I?" Rosemary persisted, with a sinking feeling.

"I'm Claire Rome." There was a little more animation in the acknowledgment but the woman's voice still sounded thready. "I—I didn't know you'd be here so soon. I thought you were still in London."

"The sample of your products really impressed the man I work for," Rosemary said, trying to put a light note into the conversation, "so I didn't waste any time coming to Cornwall. Do you think we might get together this morning so I could see a more complete selection?"

"This morning?"

The voice at the other end of the wire sounded aghast at the idea and Rosemary frowned, unable to understand the British woman's reluctance. It would have been more natural for her to have been waiting on the front steps of the Carras Hotel when an international buyer dropped in. Instead, she sounded as if Dracula had suddenly surfaced in the living room.

Rosemary took a deep breath. "I *would* like it to be soon. It's already so close to the holidays that we'll have to concentrate just on our local buyers this year. Of course, if you're not feeling well, I can make it another day."

"No—that's all right. I can get most of our sample models together in an hour or so. But I don't have a car, so you'll have to come to the house."

Curiouser and curiouser, Rosemary thought, but at least there was hope. "Will eleven be convenient?"

"Please yourself. Be sure and knock. The doorbell isn't working. My husband can't find time to fix it."

The last was said with such acrimony that Rosemary blinked. Apparently the home life of the Romes wasn't going as well as their doll business. Fortunately, it wasn't any of her affair—unless it had something to do with Claire Rome's indisposition. "I'll be there at eleven," Rosemary confirmed quietly. "It shouldn't take long. I'm looking forward to meeting you."

Rosemary shook her head after she'd hung up but decided there was no point in borrowing trouble. For the moment, it made more sense to arrange for a taxi at ten-thirty or thereabouts, but first she'd go mail her postcard as an excuse to get out in the sunny morning air.

It was easy to find the mailbox, although it was simply mounted on somebody's front gate. After Rosemary had deposited her card in the slot, she took a picture of the practical installation, mentally vowing to send it to the U. S. postal authorities the next time they claimed a budget crisis.

She continued on down the street for several blocks, enjoying the freshly washed smell of the morning and the quiet residential area of nicely maintained stone houses with steep slate roofs. When she found a tiny corner newsagent, she purchased a supply of candy bars to replenish her cache and learned from the shopkeeper that the coastal freighter had sunk in the gale during the night but that rescue units had been able to save the crew.

Mrs. Carras confirmed the report when Rosemary went back to the hotel. "Aye, it was a bad one," the older woman said, leaning on the reception counter. "I'm happy for the crew and their families. At least we won't have another Port Quinn disaster from this storm."

"What happened at Port Quinn?"

"It's easy to see you haven't been in Cornwall long," the other said with a smile, "or you'd have heard the story. Port Quinn was once a busy fishing village on our north coast. It's deserted now, but according to legend the fleet sailed out one evening and was never seen again. When a storm hits nowadays, they say you can hear the forty widows wailing on the quay where they waited for their menfolk to come back. Of course, others say it's just the cries of the seabirds. Makes a person wonder, though."

"I'd like to go there if I have time," Rosemary said, intrigued by the account. "Some of the harbors and coves that I saw from the train on the way down here looked like wonderful places to explore. Do you suppose yesterday's storm caused much damage?"

"I haven't heard of anything serious from the newscasts. Of course, it's early to tell."

"Well, from the looks of all these stone houses around here," Rosemary said, waving in the general direction of the street, "I shouldn't think that anything could disturb them."

"Oh, not here. This is high ground. But some of

the other places won't fare so well. I shouldn't wonder if that's one reason Mr. Harcourt had to leave so early—the mine could have been flooded. There's been trouble at Wheal Tamar before."

"So I understand." Rosemary was thinking of the explosion that Daniel had mentioned and reddened under Mrs. Carras' interested gaze. "I was reading a book on Cornish tin mines," she said, not bothering to mention that she'd just purchased a pamphlet on the subject along with her candy bars and had it tucked in her purse at that very moment.

"That's not surprising—your being with Mr. Harcourt and all. Is your new room all right?"

Before Rosemary could reply, a man wearing a stiff-brimmed cap opened the hotel door.

"Somebody here call a taxi for Alexandra Drive?"

"Yes, I did." Rosemary shoved the strap of her bag up more firmly on her shoulder and tightened the belt of her raincoat. "I'm all ready. See you later, Mrs. Carras."

The driver lost no time ushering his fare into the back seat of a well-worn taxi and setting off, telling Rosemary briskly that the address of the Rome house wasn't more than fifteen minutes away on the outskirts of town. "It would have taken you longer if we'd gone earlier," he said, turning onto a main motorway a little later from one of the roundabouts, or traffic circles. "All the people driving to work."

"Then the storm didn't disrupt anything in this part of town?"

"Not so you'd notice. What's one rainstorm more or less in the scheme of things?"

When they turned into the quiet suburban neighborhood on Alexandra Drive a little later, Rosemary decided the driver hadn't been exaggerating. The only evidence of the night's storm was some stray branches under the shade trees on either side of the street. The houses were considerably more modest than those on the hill near the Carras Hotel, but they were well built, with small lawns in front of them.

But, as in most neighborhoods, there was one house on the block where the stucco was blotched and the roof gutter had probably been clinging precariously long before the recent storm. The patch of lawn needed trimming and weeds were rampant around a listing metal gate by the sidewalk. Unfortunately, the taxi driver slowed to a stop directly in front of it.

"Is this the place?" Rosemary asked, her heart sinking.

"It's the number you gave me. Want me to wait while you check?"

"No—it'll be all right. I called for an appointment." Rosemary paid him and got out, but lingered by the side of the car. "Will there be any trouble getting a taxi when I'm finished?"

"Not at this time of day. You shouldn't have to wait more than ten minutes." The driver reached up and took a card from the clip on his sun visor. "Just call this number."

Rosemary watched him drive off and then

straightened her shoulders, telling herself that there
was no reason to dread the interview just because
Mrs. Rome's husband didn't mow his lawn at regular
intervals. And it wasn't surprising that the place
looked shabby; people who were rolling in money
didn't make a habit of starting cottage industries.

Rosemary opened the gate and managed to shove it
closed behind her before going up the cement walk
to the house. A nearby redwood lawn chair with
several slats missing didn't add to an atmosphere of
gracious living any more than the worn front door.
She knocked firmly and then waited.

It wasn't long before there were hurried footsteps
and it opened to reveal a willowy blonde woman of
about thirty who had red-rimmed eyes and was holding a handkerchief to her nose.

Oh, Lord, thought Rosemary even as she managed
a smile and asked, "Mrs. Rome?"

The blonde nodded and sniffed, then blew her nose
vigorously. The interval gave Rosemary a chance to
inspect her more closely. Even with her eyes swollen
from crying, the woman was attractive. Her close-
cropped hair gave a youthful piquancy to her thin
face and she had the slender grace of a high-fashion
model. Unfortunately, her worn cotton dress showed
that her life style was anything but luxurious.

"I'm sorry things are in such a mess," she said,
waving a hand to the entrance hall behind her where
Rosemary could see a table crowded with magazines,
some children's clothing, and two golf clubs atop the
pile.

"It doesn't matter a bit," Rosemary said truthfully. "I just came to see your Cornish Cuties—that *is* the name for your dolls, isn't it?"

Claire grimaced and shoved her handkerchief in the pocket of her dress. "It's not a very good trade name. We're still feeling our way, but you might as well inspect the current crop—oh, damn! That gate won't ever stay closed."

"It's my fault," Rosemary apologized, turning on the step to follow her gaze. "I thought I'd fastened it."

"I'd better do it now." Claire went past her and started down the walk. She moved slowly as if every step were an effort, and as she reached the redwood lawn chair, she swayed suddenly and clutched the back for support.

Alarmed, Rosemary hurried after her. "Is something wrong? You'd better sit down."

"Before I fall down?" The other rested her head against the back of the chair. "Oh, God, I'm so woozy."

Bending over her, Rosemary noticed the red and swollen skin along Claire's jawline. "Your face," she said in concern, "it's all bruised. Did you fall?"

A flush spread over the other's skin and she raised her head, obviously trying to make light of the situation. "Silly of me, wasn't it. I guess I should have put my head down or something. I've been feeling dizzy ever since."

"You should have called a doctor. We'll have to get

you back inside. Just hang onto me and I'll do my best to steer you . . ."

Rosemary was so intent on trying to lift Claire and get her started on the path that she almost collapsed herself when a masculine voice sounded behind her.

"Claire! What in the devil's going on? What's wrong with you?"

The woman in Rosemary's grasp stiffened and then cast herself into Simon Hardy's outstretched arms, sobbing uncontrollably.

He stared bewilderedly over her head at Rosemary's startled figure as she tried to take in this newest development. "Miss Lewis! Good Lord! What are you doing here?"

"I was about to ask the same thing," said still another deep voice.

Rosemary whirled to see a man coming through the gate. "Daniel! I mean Mr. Harcourt. Are you buying dolls, too?"

"Hardly." He pulled up at her side and looked with concern at the woman still clinging to Simon. "Mrs. Rome?" I'm a friend of Rosemary's. Can I help you back into the house?"

"If my sister needs help—I can certainly take care of it," Simon said with some asperity.

"Sorry." Daniel didn't look it, but he waited calmly for an introduction.

"This is Simon Hardy," Rosemary obliged. "He's the man I met on the train from London yesterday."

Claire made an effort to stand up straight but kept

her hold on her brother's sleeve. "I'm frightfully sorry about our appointment, Miss Lewis. I don't usually treat buyers this way. Simon will tell you that, but I've had other problems lately—"

"Which will all work out if you give them a chance," Simon cut in.

"But the important thing is to get you feeling better," Rosemary said, still worried about Claire's frailty.

"My thought exactly," Simon told his sister. "Besides, Rosemary can come around again—I'll make sure of it. Right now, I still can't get over the coincidence. Imagine, the two of us being seatmates on the train and all the while she was coming to Cornwall just to visit you, Claire."

"I hate to spoil the story," Daniel responded, possessively draping his arm about Rosemary's shoulders, "but that wasn't the only reason for her visit." He ignored Rosemary's astonished reaction and turned back to Simon. "Or the only coincidence. I gather that the Edwin Rome who works at Wheal Tamar is your brother-in-law."

"That's right." Simon kept a protective clasp on his sister as they moved back to the front door, but he lingered on the threshold. His eyes became thoughtful slits as he surveyed Daniel. "Edwin's an electrical foreman there but I don't understand what it has to do with you."

"Mr. Harcourt's a mining consultant who's working at Wheal Tamar, too," Rosemary said. She tried to slide out from under Daniel's grip but he merely tightened his fingers, making her glare up at him.

"That's right." Daniel smiled fondly down at her angry face. "Rosemary's an old friend of mine from home. Did you tell them about how we met, darling?"

She felt his warning fingers and managed a weak, "I didn't have time."

He seemed satisfied with that, turning his attention to Claire, "I gather your husband isn't home now, Mrs. Rome."

"No. He'll be at the mine if you want him."

Daniel grinned at her—a slow, slanted grin that was full of warmth. "No way. I'm playing hookey for the rest of the day and I suggest that you do the same. There's no need for you to worry about business. I can bring Rosemary back at another time when you're feeling better."

"That won't be necessary . . ." Rosemary announced, still annoyed over that casual "darling" he'd tossed into the conversation.

"Of course not," Simon agreed. "I'll be glad to furnish transportation any time. I'd planned to call you this afternoon, anyway," he told Rosemary firmly.

"Better make it tomorrow," Daniel retorted. "I plan to take her to Tintagel for the rest of the day."

"Can't I say anything?" Rosemary asked, her tone thin with suppressed anger.

"Of course, honey, but not right now." Daniel's grip on her shoulders felt like steel as his lips trailed over her cheek, finishing with a casual kiss at the corner of her mouth. "Mrs. Rome needs rest and you'll have plenty of opportunity to see her another time." He nodded to Simon and his sister and said, "It was nice meeting you both," before steering Rosemary back down the path toward the sidewalk.

"You don't have to haul me along like a piece of driftwood," she protested in a furious undertone as he paused to open the gate.

"Then behave yourself and I'll let go. Now is *not* the time to pitch a tantrum. Just turn around and smile at the nice people when you get in my car," he went on conversationally. "It's the gray one right across the street. After we're out of here, you can tell me who's been knocking that poor woman around."

Rosemary stared up at him, as if unable to believe her ears. "You mean . . ."

"I sure as hell do! It doesn't take a mastermind to figure that out. I don't know what's going on with that bunch but Claire Rome didn't just fall down—she was shoved."

Chapter Four

His pronouncement drove everything else from Rosemary's mind. "Then I wasn't imagining things," she murmured, forgetting completely about reading him a riot act over his own behavior.

"Not from my place on the sidelines." He opened the door of the small sedan and helped her into the front seat.

Rosemary looked back to the porch as Daniel went around the car to get behind the steering wheel, catching Simon delivering a thoughtful look in their direction just before he closed the front door. "Well, at least Simon couldn't have been to blame," she said when Daniel had started the car and they were headed back toward the highway.

"What makes you say that?"

"She fell into his arms—that's why. And she certainly wouldn't have wanted to go back into the house with him if she'd been scared to death."

"Don't get things all out of proportion. We're talking about a minor domestic fracas—not a case of Jack the Ripper."

"Then you think it was her husband?"

"Probably. If it had been a stranger who roughed her up, she would have called the police—not stood around weeping."

"She could have a gentleman friend," Rosemary said, trying to consider all the possibilities.

"Use your head. Nobody would schedule an illicit liaison on a split-second itinerary."

"You sound as if you know all about it," she felt compelled to tell him.

"Oh, sure. I had to fit Mrs. Carras in between breakfast and Wheal Tamar just this morning."

She snorted disdainfully and waited for him to make a left turn onto the main road, heading back toward the center of town before she added, "I suppose you have an equally convincing explanation for your behavior back there. It's not that I don't appreciate your concern, Mr. Harcourt, but . . ."

"You can scrub that dialogue," he said, interrupting her ruthlessly.

"Do what?"

"Stop the Mr. Harcourt stuff. Just because you're in Cornwall doesn't mean you have to sound like a Jane Austen character."

"You have a nerve—telling me what to do. Especially after showing up uninvited and dragging me off." She gave his profile an angry glance. "How did you know I was even there?"

"What makes you think I was calling on you?" he drawled with amusement. "Hasn't it occurred to you that maybe my business was with Edwin Rome?"

His cool snub brought color to her cheeks. "I'm sorry," she said finally. "I didn't stop to think."

A flicker of a smile softened his stern expression. "I should let you suffer a while, but as long as we're being honest, I'll come clean. I didn't have any intention of seeing the elusive Mr. Rome. In fact, I'd already checked that he was on the job at the mine this morning."

"Then what were you doing at his house?"

"Picking you up," he replied offhandedly. "You forgot to leave a message at the hotel but it wasn't hard to follow you. Mrs. Carras told me you'd taken a cab."

"You've arranged quite an early-warning system, haven't you?" she said icily, not at all pleased by his steamroller tactics.

"It saves considerable time." He slowed for a traffic circle and gave her a sideways glance that had no apology in it. "Do you want to visit Tintagel today or don't you?"

In the pause that followed, Rosemary searched for an answer that would salvage her pride but still give her the chance to see Cornwall's premier tourist attraction.

Daniel must have sensed her indecision, because he finally said solemnly, "I'd be pleased if you'd come along."

"Thank you, I'd love to," she said, knowing that

she hadn't fooled him in the least. "Are we on the way there now?"

"We'd better get something to eat first. There isn't much in that line around the castle. As a matter of fact, there isn't much around here, either." He frowned and added, "We could go back to the hotel but it will take more time."

"I'd rather skip the calories. Anything will do."

"That might be about what you'll get. There's a leisure park up the road that has food but it won't ever make the Michelin guide."

"That doesn't matter. At least it's something different. What is a leisure park anyway?"

"If you combine a grease joint, a stab at an amusement park for the kiddies, and some flower beds—it comes out a leisure park in this part of the world."

"Oh." She looked dismayed for a moment and then rallied. "Will they have clotted cream and Cornish pasties?"

He grinned. "You've been reading the right books, but don't hold your breath. At least there'll be a cup of tea and a package of biscuits to stave off starvation."

Rosemary sat back, satisfied. She approved of his new-found consideration but she was still reluctant to let him escape completely unscathed after that possessive takeover at the Rome house. She knew it had been deliberate and that Simon was left wondering whether he should infringe on another man's property for the rest of her stay. While she wasn't interested in a permanent relationship with Simon,

she certainly had no intention of having Daniel
think he was the only man in her life while she was
in Cornwall.

She let a few more miles of highway pass while
she thought that over, waiting until they reached a
sign announcing that the leisure park was just a
quarter-mile away when she said, "We'd better get a
few things settled before we go in."

"That has an ominous sound." Despite his words,
Daniel didn't look particularly worried. "What's on
your mind now?"

"Just that I intend to pay my own lunch bill—for
one thing."

"I see." There was a slight pause, then, "What do
you want to do about the gas?"

Of all the possible replies he could have made, that
one left her stunned to silence. He'd swung left into
the gravel drive leading to a sprawling group of
buildings and braked alongside a charter bus before
she probed hesitantly, "I don't quite know what you
mean. What about the gas?"

"I thought that you'd probably want to split the
mileage costs, too." Daniel turned off the ignition
and dropped the key in his pocket. "Then there'll be
the admission and the parking fees at the castle. It
might be easier if I pay everything as we go along
and we can settle the account later."

Rosemary felt she could afford to be gracious since
he was so logical about it. There was no way she
could account for the niggling feeling of disappointment that had followed his words. She took a deep

breath and tried another subject. "As long as we're setting up house rules, I'd like to get another thing straight. You may have needed an excuse for appearing at the Rome's, but after this—don't drag me into it."

"I don't quite know what you mean."

"I should think it would be obvious." The words were out before she realized that he was mimicking her earlier retort. That knowledge made her voice even more stilted. "I mean that it won't be necessary to act as if we were old friends. When I see Simon again, I can explain so he won't get the wrong idea.".

"You mean because I had my arm around you?" Daniel's eyebrows went up.

"Well, that—and other things." There was a pause, but when he didn't do anything to break it, she blurted out, "You didn't have to kiss me."

"Good Lord! That peck on the cheek! You call that a kiss?" There was no hiding the laughter in his voice by then.

"I don't intend to discuss it any further," Rosemary said and reached for the car door handle.

Daniel's hand clamped over hers, effectively pinning her in her seat. "No. You're the one who insisted on getting things straight." He shifted to pull her toward him before she realized what was happening. "Now this is the kind of a peck I gave you on the Romes' front lawn." Ignoring her startled, wide-eyed glance, he bent to brush his lips over the corner of her mouth. Even as she tried to pull back, his clasp tightened and he crushed her tight against his chest, letting her feel his strength. "If you're going to complain about being kissed, then we'd better both be talking about the same thing."

From the moment his mouth parted her lips, Daniel abandoned any elementary instruction and plunged into postgraduate expertise. His approach was teasing, sensual, and utterly devastating—making her forget everything except his hard body next to hers. His hands worked a special magic as they slid caressingly down from her shoulders, leaving every nerve ending she possessed quivering with awareness and delight.

Then, abruptly, he pulled away and propped her against the seat as he said, "That's more what I had in mind. But naturally, if it upsets you—it won't happen again. Let's go in and have lunch."

Mercifully, he got out of the car without looking back, so he didn't see Rosemary make two attempts with a trembling hand to open her door. She was breathing hard and it was a tossup whether her knees would support her when her feet reached the ground, but she would have committed hara-kiri on the spot before she would have mentioned it.

She trailed behind his tall figure to the entrance, wondering how she'd ever get through the lunch ahead.

It was his air of total unconcern that saved her. He waited solicitously at the end of the line in the cafeteria and ushered her in front of him as he might have someone in knee socks.

Rosemary was still so unnerved that she ended up

with a tired-looking scone on her tray as well as the pasty she'd meant to try. After that, it was a foregone conclusion that she'd spill her tea into her saucer and need another napkin for mopping it up. By the time they reached an unoccupied table and sat down, she knew she'd aged five years.

Daniel provided a welcome diversion by announcing that the souvenir shop at the end of the room was a good source for reference books on Cornwall. "If you're really interested in the place."

"I'll probably wait until I get back to London," she told him, trying to sound as if Cornish history were vital to her existence. "My overnight case is already bulging and I may have some of Claire's dolls to carry, too."

Daniel nodded and inspected his cheese sandwich with casual interest before taking a bite. Rosemary decided that she'd better tackle her Cornish pasty while it was still lukewarm. Unfortunately, her plastic fork barely dented the crust when she made the attempt.

"Might as well pick it up," Daniel advised, noting her dismay. "There's nobody here to impress."

"It's not that. I'd just rather not have the gravy run down my arm."

"You won't have to worry about that," he said, fatalistically. "I've eaten here before."

"But it's supposed to be potatoes and beef in gravy with a touch of onion—" she began and then shrugged, finally taking a bite from the end.

From across the table, Daniel observed her deflated

expression. "I didn't think gravy would be a problem. Would you like part of my sandwich?"

"Oh, no thanks." She was peering into the pasty. "This really isn't so bad. There's potatoe and some kind of meat—"

"I wouldn't dwell on it. Just don't give up on Cornish food because of this place. I imagine there are still some wonderful pasties made around here if we only knew how to find them."

"Even the tourist guidebooks say that the days of finding a pasty where one end is filled with sliced apples for dessert are gone forever."

"Like the old-time pilchard pies."

"Pilchard are fish, aren't they?"

"That's right. And any cook who knew her stuff left the fish heads on, peering out through the top crust."

Rosemary shuddered visibly. "It sounds like a close relation to fishhead stew. I knew a Norwegian once who made that last for a week."

"It would last a lot longer in my house."

She smiled and took another bite of the lukewarm pasty, only to put it down with finality. "I think I'll go on to dessert."

She managed to consume the scone, and washed it down with the piping hot tea. It was an effort to eat anything but she was darned if she'd let on that her stomach muscles were still in knots after his demonstration in the car park.

As soon as she put down her cup, Daniel shoved back his chair. "If you're finished, we'll be on our way. It takes a while to get up the coast, though there shouldn't be much traffic at this season."

She followed him out of the cafeteria, giving a wide margin to the souvenir shop, which featured everything from ceramic pasties to seashell lamp shades. "I haven't seen a traffic jam anywhere in Cornwall."

"Be thankful you're not here in the summer holidays." Daniel was opening her car door as he spoke. "For the Englishman, Cornwall is Florida, Coney Island, and Malibu rolled into one. You'll see what I mean on the way to Tintagel. We pass one beach resort after the other and in season they'd be crammed to the rafters." Noting her dismayed expression, he grinned. "You're not the first American to come here and be confused by modern-day Cornwall."

"I'm not so sure that I want to be disillusioned," she admitted as he got in and started the car. "Next you'll be telling me that it wasn't true about the coast watchers and wreckers who tied lanterns to the tails of their cows during storms."

"Hoping that when the animals walked along the clifftops at night the sea captains would think the swaying lights came from ships' masts?"

"And steer their ships onto the rocks as a result," she finished for him. "We read the same novels."

"Or saw the same movie." He swung onto the main road again, but when they'd retraced their route to the roundabout, he took another, narrower road and headed northwest toward the coast. "It makes a good story but don't count on it as the gospel. There's no doubt that there were wreckers aplenty when word came that a vessel was in trouble. Apparently crowds would follow the stricken ship, just waiting for it to pile up on the rocks.

"So they could save the crew?"

"There might have been some who had that in mind but most people were just intent on getting everything off the wreck before it foundered completely. They'd salvage cabin doors, timbers—anything they could haul in addition to the cargo. Apparently, the ships wrecked along the north coast in the eighteenth century had usually sailed from Ireland, so they'd be carrying butter and bacon. On the south coast, the French ships would have a cargo of cloth, or better still, a hold full of wine. Very little of it ever reached Customs."

"I suppose you know that you're destroying illusions right and left."

He grinned at her aggrieved tone. "You can keep a few intact along with the other citizens here. They're probably still believing in Madgy Figgy and all her powers."

"Who on earth was Madgy Figgy?"

"An authentic, dues-paying witch, if all the legends are to be credited. Apparently she sat in a rock chair near the headland and summoned storms to cause the shipwrecks. After the vessels were driven on the rocks, she flew off on a stalk of ragwort— laughing fit to kill."

"Now that's a bit too much to swallow."

Daniel shrugged. "In that case you won't be going to Logan Rock."

Rosemary bestowed a thoughtful glance on him. "I feel like a straight man in this routine. Exactly why won't I be visiting Logan Rock—wherever it is?"

"Down by Porthcurno Bay—close to Land's End. And you'd better skip the Rock because that's where aspiring witches go these days."

"You're kidding!"

He held up his palm as if taking a vow. "Scout's honor. All you have to do is touch Logan Rock nine times at midnight."

"And?"

Daniel snapped his fingers. "Instant Madgy Figgy."

Rosemary shook her head, bemused. Such stories seemed incongruous on a peaceful afternoon with pale sunshine bathing the landscape around them. The green fields on either side of the road were neatly bisected with hedgerows of Cornish stone, and scattered farm dwellings on the smallholdings were constructed of the same gray granite. The buildings were almost always two-storied, with straight, unobtrusive lines and, except for color, looked incredibly like the little block houses that came in a Monopoly® set.

Finally, the road edged a cliff and Rosemary had her first glimpse of the ocean far below.

The scene showed clearly how the Cornishmen must have struggled to exist in such barren surroundings over the years. And, remembering the ferocity of the storm, she could easily understand how those endless miles of rocks and cliffs could spell disaster.

"You look as if you're about to cry."

Daniel's comment roused her and she turned quickly to face him, shaking her head. "Not really. I was just thinking about what's happened in this part of the world. There's something about the countryside that defies the twentieth century."

He gave her a disarming grin. "I found that out the first day I checked in at the mine, and I thought I was the practical type."

"I'd really like to see a Cornish tin mine. Are we anywhere near your Wheal Tamar?"

"Not close enough if we want to see Tintagel properly. There is another mine not far from here that's similar in general layout. We could detour by it and then maybe you can have a guided tour of Wheal Tamar another day."

"That would be wonderful!"

He nodded as if pleased and somewhat surprised by her enthusiasm. "It's not very exciting or beautiful. Mines seldom are—but you'll see that for yourself. Maybe you noticed some of the empty 'castles' on the way to Truro." When she stared at him, puzzled, he went on to explain. "There are a lot of derelict stone buildings on hillsides around here that were once part of the mines."

"Were they always searching for tin?" she asked, as he slowed for another traffic circle and then took a winding road that led back inland.

"Nope. Over the years, they tried for tungsten, arsenic, and copper." As she started to laugh, he asked quizzically. "Now what?"

"It's just that I never thought of arsenic being mined."

"I know. It only appears in bottles on the drugstore shelf."

"Or in bags in the gardener's shed," she confessed, delighted that he tuned into her wavelength without trouble. "Just in time for the villain to spoon some out in a murder mystery."

He grinned disarmingly. "Well, Cornwall was the beginning of it, but if you're harboring any thoughts along that line—you'll have to postpone them. The mine we're going to see now was strictly tin and they've even closed the operation down. Ran out of money a few months back." He slowed and pulled off onto the narrow shoulder of the road so that he could brake and let Rosemary view the scene properly. "I warned you that it wasn't very exciting."

"Good Lord, I don't need things sugar-coated. Tell me about it. What's that tall thing—that's sort of like an oil derrick? It must be a hundred feet high at least."

As he leaned over to see where she was pointing, she felt his thigh brush hers and she drew in her breath sharply, remembering what had happened the last time he'd been that close.

Apparently Daniel didn't clutter his mind with such trivia, because he just said, "It's called a headframe. It's made up of crisscrossed steel I-beams with a two-inch cable for a pulley that goes over the shaft. The cable wraps around a horizontal hoist spool just beyond."

"How about the shaft? How deep does it go?"

"It depends. Anywhere in the two thousand to four thousand foot range."

Her mouth dropped open. "I had no idea."

He nodded. "If you really want to get warm in Cornwall—head straight down. The temperature in the working areas is well over a hundred degrees. Even when they're under the ocean."

"You mean the miners work under water, too?"

"If necessary. There was one mine out by Land's End that was worked nine hundred feet below sea level."

"I couldn't do that," she said frankly after thinking it over. "I'd have claustrophobia before I ever went down the shaft."

"It helps if you close your eyes."

She stared incredulously until she saw a grin soften his features. Then she shook her head reprovingly and turned back to the mine on the hillside. "What about the rest of the buildings?" she asked, gesturing toward some low stone structures huddled on the rocky hill.

"The small one was probably the office. The bigger one up on the side of the hill is the mill. That's where they'd crush the ore and remove the tin-containing minerals."

"What about those huts—the ones with metal siding?"

"Just outbuildings. Don't forget, when this mine was working—there would have been three to five hundred miners, so it wasn't a small operation." He straightened behind the wheel again, reaching for the ignition key.

"And Wheal Tamar? The place where you're working? Is it as big?"

"About the same." He started the engine and pulled out onto the nearly deserted highway, looking for a place to make a U-turn. "And almost in the same condition. It's going to take some doing to keep the place functioning."

"I don't imagine that explosion helped the cause," she said sympathetically. "When things go wrong, it's like the start of a landslide."

"That might be the general rule but I doubt if it applies in this case," he said in a grim tone as he managed to find room to turn and head the car back toward the coast. "At Wheal Tamar I'm almost sure the damage has been deliberate. Unfortunately, unless I can pin down who or what's to blame damned fast—the owners will have to close or sell out. That's why they retained our firm. Lance had just gotten married when they contacted us, so I offered to take the job."

"Lance told me about that. And from what I saw of the two of them—he and Gwen aren't missing Cornwall one bit."

"So I hear—" he broke off to swear as a cyclist swerved out in front of the car from a farm driveway. "All the nuts around aren't in Wheal Tamar," he said afterwards with an apologetic look in her direction.

"He's lucky you missed him." She turned to face him more squarely. "Tell me more about those mine explosions."

"Well, there've been two this month. The first wasn't as big as this last one."

"But they weren't the only reason that your firm was called in?"

"Let's say a contributing cause. The big thing is that Wheal Tamar simply isn't paying off according to formula."

"How can you tell?"

"Strict mathematics. The amount of metal extracted wasn't as much as the grade of ore times the tonnage mined warranted."

"Whoa—you'll have to make allowances for me. I had trouble with long division."

He shot her a skeptical glance but merely said, "In my opinion, there's been some creative bookkeeping on the mine accounts. I've suggested the directors hire another accounting firm to check the figures and another exploration team to reassess the mine's potential."

Rosemary frowned. "Even so—crooked accountants wouldn't go around blowing things up—unless the British do things differently."

"That's why I want to interview Claire Rome's husband. As an electrical foreman, he should be able to pinpoint the cause of this last explosion. I couldn't see him before because he's been off work this past week—until today. The flu or something."

"And now his wife looks as if she's fallen down the stairs except—"

"She lives in a one-story house," Daniel finished for her. "Of course, there could be a perfectly simple explanation. Maybe your friend Simon will furnish one. He seemed to be pretty close to his sister."

"That's not surprising," Rosemary replied, feeling that Simon deserved some defense. "Mrs. Rome will probably clear up the mystery herself when I see her again. I can't think the family's involved in anything shady. She wouldn't be trying for extra money by making dolls if they were tapping Wheal Tamar for—" she paused to find the right words.

"Ill-gotten gains?"

She smiled reluctantly. "Something like that."

"Time will tell. Not too much time, though. I'd planned to be finished here before this." He made no attempt to break the silence that followed, seemingly intent on the winding two-lane road which was leading them back to the coast.

The traffic thickened as they turned northward about five minutes later to follow a highway sign marked "Tintagel."

"I'm not so sure that we've seen the last of the storm," Daniel said with a perturbed glance at some clouds scudding in from the Atlantic. "At least we should have time for a short tour of the castle. We'll probably still get our feet wet—the paths are mostly dirt and gravel, so the mud's going to be thick after last night's rain. I hope you're prepared."

"As much as I'll ever be," Rosemary replied, waggling her low-heeled pumps. "Boots take up too much room in a suitcase. Tell me, is this place the real thing? Was this truly where King Arthur had his Round Table?"

"It depends on who you ask. The local tour guides swear to it. They even claim that the village of Camelford nearby is the original Camelot."

"You don't sound convinced."

He shrugged and slowed the car as they entered a small village which seemed mainly composed of antique shops, souvenir shops, and hole-in-the-wall eating places. "It doesn't really matter. The ruins are worth seeing whether King Arthur lived here or just some poor prisoners in the fifteenth century. At least they all had a view," he said, nodding toward the famous ruin, which was up on a cliff overlooking the sea just ahead of them. "We'll have to leave the car in this lot and walk the rest of the way."

Rosemary peered eagerly at the landmark, hardly aware of the parking attendant who was waiting to collect his fee once Daniel had turned off the ignition.

When their business was finished, Daniel reached under the seat for his camera and opened his car door. "Better put on that nylon raincoat of yours to keep warm," he told Rosemary. "Is there a scarf in the pocket?" When she nodded, he added, "You'll need it. The wind really whistles up on top."

She nodded and frowned as she struggled to get the strap of her heavy purse on her shoulder, once out of the car.

"Unless you're passionately attached to that thing, I can lock it in the trunk," Daniel offered.

"That would help. I'm already lopsided after carrying it for a week." She handed it to him so he could stow it away. "That's marvelous! Now I'm ready for anything. Where do we go first?"

"Down this gravel path to the ocean. Or there's a Land Rover that makes the trip about every half hour—if you'd rather wait."

"Oh, no." She cast an anxious look at the sky, which was becoming more overcast all the time. "Let's not waste a minute."

His expression lightened. "Fair enough. Hang on to me in the steep places. I'd hate to lose you off the cliff before you had a chance to spit over the stone wall up at the top."

She gave a gurgle of laughter. "It's nice to know that you don't have any dastardly schemes to get rid of me. I didn't think those castle ruins would be on such a cliff or that the place would be so deserted."

"Blame that on the season and the weather." He steered her down the steep pathway, trying to find some solid layers of gravel so they could avoid the squelchy patches of mud. "Probably if we'd any sense, we would have waited until things dried out a bit."

Her gaze followed the switchback trail which

went up the steep hillside to the ruins. "At least there's a railing on parts of it so we won't slip off."

"You sound nice and sensible about the whole idea," he approved. "Some women I know would never have left the car. I gather that heights don't bother you?"

"Not really," she said, crossing her fingers surreptitiously. "Tell me about this place," she went on, hoping to get their conversation on a more cheerful aspect. "There must have been a reason for building it on the edge of nothing."

"Sheer preservation. In the twelfth century, neighbors dropped in uninvited and very frequently they'd also drop their host off the nearest cliff if they liked his real estate."

"Charming," Rosemary murmured, wishing that she could sit down and catch her breath before they started the arduous climb in front of them. Fortunately, just then they came upon a ticket booth and she sank onto a flat boulder, while Daniel went to pay their admission. "I must remember how much I owe you when we're finished with all this," she said as he came back. "There's the parking fee, too."

"I'm glad you reminded me." He kept his tone solemn. "I'd planned on volunteering my services as a guide at the top—if that doesn't upset you."

She shot him a suspicious glance as she pushed upright again. "Not at all. Would you like to rest here for a moment?"

He immediately shook his head. "There's no use

wasting time. Unless you're tired?" The last was tacked on negligently.

"No, of course not." Rosemary managed a brilliant smile. "Lead on—I'll be right behind you."

"It might be better the other way around." He gestured toward the steep path, which was wide enough only for one person. "This way, I can hang on to you if need be."

"You make it sound like going up Everest," Rosemary protested, but started toward the track. She let her hand hover over the wooden railing at the side, trying to give an appearance of nonchalance when in reality the first glimpse down had made her want to cling with both hands, and her teeth as well.

There wasn't any conversation after that. For one thing, she didn't have breath to spare, and she was so intent on not making a misstep on the switchback path that every other thought was driven from her mind.

After they'd completed the first part of the climb, Daniel was discreetly silent as she lingered at the halfway point. She tried to hide her exhaustion as she leaned against the sheer wall, but when she took a deep breath, she was sure that she sounded like a beached whale.

He displayed tremendous tact in ignoring her panting form, looking instead at the rugged rock coastline below. "It must have been hard on the prisoners if they had any hopes of escape," he said idly, leaning against the flat rock beside her and shielding her from the wind in the process.

That helped so much that Rosemary decided to prolong the rest stop. "What prisoners? I didn't know King Arthur went in for that sort of thing."

"This wasn't legend, it was fact. In the fifteenth century, the first Duke of Cornwall died and this was used as a state prison. After another hundred years, the whole place started crumbling away. I imagine the view was the only thing left by then."

Rosemary shuddered involuntarily as she watched a wave smash over a rocky finger far below. The scene was beautiful but incredibly stark and primitive. There wasn't a softened edge to be seen; the granite cliff was sheer and sharp, the surf pounded onto the rocks with sledgehammer force, and even the wind flattened the sparse vegetation with a vengeance.

"Merlin's Cave is down at the bottom of the cliff," Daniel said, straightening to gesture in that direction.

"I'll take your word for it." Rosemary looked up the path and decided that she couldn't stall any longer. "You're sure that you don't want to go first?"

His lips quirked but he merely shook his head and waited for her to start off again.

Fortunately, the rest of the climb was easier, and when they finally reached the level area at the top, Rosemary was able to say, "I have my own idea why they built these places on the top of a cliff."

Daniel grinned and scraped his shoe on a handy patch of grass, trying to dislodge some mud from the sole. "What's that?"

"If anybody were silly enough to invade, half the soldiers would go down with heart attacks on the hike up and the rest of them would have a stroke when they finally arrived."

He pursed his lips as if considering it. "Very likely," he said finally. "But think what a saving on the boiling oil!"

She wandered across to the remaining bits of stone battlement and peeked over the cliff before stepping prudently back onto a tiny patch of lawn. "It seems strange to see this," she said, gesturing at the unexpected bit of green.

"Another part of the legend. The blood spilt from Excalibur is supposed to keep it thriving."

"The magic sword?"

"That's right. Apparently the turf has survived through the centuries and there aren't any springs up here."

"If I stayed in Cornwall very long, I'd be looking over my shoulder for ghosts and listening for strange voices in the fog."

"The remedy for that is a nice cup of hot coffee— if there is such a thing down in the village. How about posing against that wall while I take your picture and then we'll head back. The weather isn't getting any better and I don't fancy that path in a rainstorm."

It was a very convincing argument, and they were at the foot of the cliff twenty minutes later. This time they were lucky enough to find the Land Rover all ready to set out for the parking lot and hopped aboard. Rosemary savored every minute of the bumpy ride as the Rover ground up the steep pathway.

"I suppose this is cheating," she confessed to Daniel as they neared the top, "but I was beginning to feel frostbitten on the edges. That wind is colder than I thought." As the car emerged at the top, she glanced across the road, where she'd seen a tea shop when they'd arrived. "It looks as if we might have to postpone that coffee."

Daniel frowned as he helped her out of the Rover and nodded to the driver. "Damn! I wonder if this is early closing day. It didn't occur to me to ask."

"You couldn't know." Rosemary fell into step beside him as they made their way to the parking area where their car was one of three left on the lot. "It looks as if the attendant went home for tea, too."

"I wish he'd stuck around so we could have asked if there were another restaurant close by. Or, if I'd really used my head, I would have asked Mrs. Carras for a hotel thermos." He retrieved Rosemary's purse from the trunk and handed it over before unlocking the car door and gesturing her inside.

She waited for him to get behind the wheel. "We won't starve if we miss afternoon tea. I'm just sorry I didn't stop for a postcard on the way down while that newsagent was open. They'll have them in Truro, though."

"I'd offer to take you shopping tomorrow if I could. Unfortunately, I'm going to be busy."

His polite announcement confirmed what Rosemary had already feared; he'd taken her on as another responsibility. Not that he could do much else when his business partner had blithely made the arrangement. That realization made her tone coolly polite. "Really, you don't have to worry about me. I'm perfectly capable of hiring a car on my own, and if I see Claire Rome tomorrow—I can ask her about the other tourist sights. It's quite possible that Simon will have some ideas on that line, too. Not that it's necessary to have a man along—what are you doing?"

Her indignant query came when Daniel caught her chin in his fingers and turned her to face him on the seat. His expression was sternly forbidding, and if she hadn't already been shivering from the cold, the glare in his gray eyes would have done the trick.

"I'd rather you stayed away from Simon Hardy," he commanded, his words like chips of ice.

"For heaven's sakes, why? There's nothing wrong with the man. He was charming to me on the train and now that I'll be doing business with his sister— I certainly can't offend him."

It was hard to keep her voice from trembling when Daniel's fingers stayed firm along her jaw. And they weren't the only part of him to upset her equilibrium. In the confines of the small car, his shoulders took up more than his share of the front seat and she caught a lingering whiff of his sandalwood after-shave as he bent his head. There was no way he could have missed the rapid pulse in her throat, confirming that she was nowhere near as unaffected by his presence as she let on.

"Would you mind taking your hand away?" she said finally, trying to pull back when she couldn't outstare him. "I don't appreciate being mauled."

He gave a brief snort and lowered his hand, but took his time about it. "Lady, you don't know the meaning of the word, but if you keep on the way you're going—you'll damn well find out. Just remember that I don't have time to pull you out when you get beyond your depth with friend Simon."

She pushed back into her corner, deliberately getting as far away from him as possible. "I'm an excellent swimmer, thanks."

"Why does a woman always need the last word?" he asked scathingly as he turned to start the car.

Rosemary refrained from reminding him that she didn't get it and stared stonily through the windshield. She was darned if she could understand why Daniel's mood had changed so abruptly—especially when they'd been getting along so well. As they drove out of the parking lot, the gravel spurting from their wheels, she decided it was fortunate the tea shop *was* closed. Otherwise, they would have been staring unhappily across the table at each other, trying to ignore a silence which was bad enough in the privacy of the car.

She sneaked a glance at his rocklike profile and abandoned any attempt at an olive branch. The way his jaw was clenched, it was doubtful if he'd even be able to respond.

It was a bedraggled farm cat which abruptly resolved the dilemma five minutes later. The small animal dashed out from a fence border directly in front of their car.

Daniel swore and wrenched at the steering column. Their front wheel lurched off the surface of the road down onto a muddy shoulder, throwing Rosemary painfully against her side window.

Daniel managed to keep control of the car until it stopped, and they both watched the terrified cat streak up the other side of the road into some weeds.

"Dammit all to hell!" Daniel ground out. He switched off the ignition with a movement that threatened to bend the key and turned to appraise her. "Are you all right?"

She rubbed her temple, but nodded as she straightened. "I didn't hit hard. I don't see how you missed him." As he started to open his door, she stared perplexedly. "Why are we stopping here? You aren't hurt, are you?"

"I'm not, but I can't say the same for the front tire. Didn't you feel it go when we hit the shoulder?"

She shook her head and then watched him walk around the hood of the car to examine the tire. When he came back to slide behind the wheel, she asked, "What's the matter? Aren't you going to change it?"

He sighed as he started the motor again. "There isn't room on the shoulder, and I can't block the road. If another car comes along, we might not be as lucky as the cat. I'll have to stop at the first wide spot we come to."

"That won't help the tire, will it?" she asked, as they lurched slowly down the road.

"It's a complete write-off, anyhow. Let's hope the rim holds out." He sounded grimmer than ever as they passed another stone fence and finally pulled into the driveway of a small farm.

"I take it that we do have a spare?"

"We did when we started out." He turned off the engine and opened his door. "We should be all right unless we need more than one."

"What do you mean?"

"Just that. It didn't help that we had to go off the road, but the tire would have blown anyway. It had been slashed deliberately. Probably at that car park. Just cross your fingers that whoever it was didn't try his talents on the rest of our rubber. Otherwise you'll be a little late getting home."

"But why?" she wailed, following him back to the trunk as he reached in for the jack. "Why on earth would anyone do such a thing?"

"God knows. Maybe it was some local. On the other hand, don't forget that your friend Simon Hardy was one of the few people who knew we were going to be at Tintagel today. I'm wondering if he decided to trail along, too."

Rosemary stared at him wide-eyed. "That's ridiculous! Why would he be involved?"

Daniel shrugged, sidestepping her as he carried the jack to the front of the car. "I don't know that he is, but it's a possibility. At any rate, you'll have plenty of time to think it over while I change this damn tire." He glanced upward as he felt some drops of water on his face. "Rain!" he went on disgustedly. "That's all I need."

"I'm surprised you're not trying to blame Simon for it, as well," Rosemary told him. "Or that witch called Madgy Figgy. It would make about as much sense."

He pulled at an imaginary forelock. "Thanks very much, but you can skip your editorial opinions. If you don't belt up, you'll be hitching a ride back to Truro in the rain." He smiled grimly. "One of the unadvertised tourist attractions in Cornwall."

Chapter Five

It was an absurd attitude for a grown man to take. Rosemary let him know her feelings by a disdainful sniff as soon as he finished changing the tire and got back into the car. She stopped at that, however, as he was thoroughly out of sorts because the rain hadn't let up. It would have taken very little for his temper to flare and while she doubted his threat to leave her at the side of the road—she wasn't taking any chances. Instead, she remained politely aloof on the return drive.

They had scarcely pulled into the hotel's parking lot before she had her hand on the car door handle, saying, "Thank you for taking me. I did enjoy seeing the castle and I'm sorry that you had to get so wet changing the tire."

"Forget it," he replied brusquely. "I suppose I owe you an apology for losing my temper." He rubbed the back of his neck as if trying to ease tired muscles. "Diplomacy's not one of my long suits. I wish you'd watch your step, though. There are too damned many crazy things going on around here."

It was a reasonable request and Rosemary couldn't fault it. Especially when he kept that direct gray-eyed glance on her. "I'll be careful," she promised. Then, when he made no attempt to turn off the ignition, she asked, "Aren't you coming in?"

"Not now. I want to see about replacing the spare or getting another car before the rental agency closes. Tell Mrs. Carras not to count on me for dinner. And while I don't expect you to leave an itinerary," he said with a rueful grimace, "it wouldn't hurt to let somebody know where you're going to be tomorrow."

When Rosemary nodded hesitantly, he gave her a half-smile and drove off as soon as she got out and closed the door.

His mild warning was enough to make her decide that she'd have an early night and see if things looked better in the morning. She ate by herself in the dining room, consuming her poached fish absent-mindedly and toying with a sherry trifle afterwards. Even her new sleeping quarters weren't enough to buoy her spirits for long, and when she peeked into Daniel's room through the connecting bathroom door—she wasn't surprised to find it deserted. She retreated to her own quarters, undecided whether to lock the door on her side when she went to bed. She finally left it unlocked, knowing very well that Daniel wouldn't have been guilty of the curiosity she'd shown minutes before.

That acknowledgment didn't help her get to sleep. In fact, she was still waiting to hear some noise from his quarters an hour and a half later when she finally turned off the radio by her bed. At least there wasn't anyone to witness her idiocy, she told herself, trying to find a comforting thought.

As a result of such soul-searching, she slept lightly and woke early the next morning. The temperature had dropped during the night and she was half-frozen under her thin blanket. A hot shower would help, she decided, as she stretched and rooted for her slippers at the edge of the bed. When she carefully opened the bathroom door, she was disappointed to see a damp, crooked towel on the fixture by the tub—showing that Daniel had already come and gone. Unless he was still getting dressed . . .

She turned on the shower, waiting hopefully for a brisk knock on his connecting door and a possible invitation to breakfast. When it wasn't forthcoming, she finally bathed and got dressed, discovering as she reached the dining room that he'd already been in for coffee and gone on his way.

"That attractive blonde woman called for him," Mrs. Carras said as she led Rosemary to a table by the window. "She's been here before, so I'm pretty sure she works at Wheal Tamar. Mind you, if she were my daughter, I wouldn't let her run around in such tight clothes but these days—" She shrugged ample shoulders. "Girls please themselves."

"I doubt if Mr. Harcourt raised any objections."

"Not likely. They're all the same way—no matter what country they're from."

Her observation didn't do anything to improve

Rosemary's appetite. Nor did the prospect of a long, empty day ahead. She did feel more cheerful at the end of her breakfast when Mrs. Carras came to announce, "A telephone call, Miss Lewis. Some gentleman who wouldn't give his name."

"I'll be right there, thanks." Rosemary swallowed the last morsel of fried bread hurriedly. Dabbing at her lips with her napkin, she followed in the hotel manager's wake to pick up the receiver. "Hullo—"

"Is that you, Rosemary? Simon here. I was afraid that I might have missed you."

"I would have checked with your sister before I went out," she told him truthfully. "Is she feeling better today?"

"Practically top of the mark. A little rest was all she needed. She'd like to see you tomorrow morning if that's convenient."

Rosemary, who had been hoping for an appointment in the next hour or so, swallowed and then said, "That should be fine. What time?"

"How about my picking you up around tennish so you and Claire can get all your business over early?"

His jocular tone intimated that he wasn't taking the doll trade very seriously. Rosemary frowned, saying carefully, "It's her inventory that concerns me and what's available for the holidays. I'll have to let my firm know as soon as possible."

"I'll tell her," Simon promised. "Afterwards, I'd like to take you to lunch. There's a tolerable place in Mousehole that all the tourists like." He pronounced it "Maw-zel" but Rosemary had read enough on the quaint fishing village with the intriguing name to identify it.

"I had planned to take a peek at the town while I was here," she confessed.

"What better way than over lunch?" he retorted cheerfully. "I'll make reservations now so we can get a nice window table."

"That sounds wonderful. Will Claire be joining us?"

"She would be if I asked her, but I didn't plan on it," he replied with brotherly candor. "Business first, pleasure later—that's my motto. All right with you?"

He sounded so cheerful that Rosemary had to smile. "Of course."

"Maybe I should ask if your chap Harcourt will be along?" Simon said after a moment's pause.

"I didn't plan on it," she mimicked. "And he's not—" Somehow she couldn't bring herself to say "my chap" and substituted "generally free during the day."

"Working at the mine, is he?"

"I guess so. He didn't tell me what his schedule was going to be. If you're really interested perhaps your brother-in-law would know."

There was a distinct pause. Then Simon said, "Why should he?"

"Well, since they're both working at Wheal Tamar . . ." By then, Rosemary was sorry she'd brought the subject up.

Simon must have felt the same way. His tone was wry as he said, "Edwin doesn't mix with the management blokes. The only reason he even heard of Harcourt was because of the explosion. Apparently Harcourt was asking questions of everybody he could find."

"I see."

When she didn't offer any more, Simon said, "Well, then—I'll see you tomorrow at ten."

"Thanks very much. I'll look forward to it," she responded politely. After Simon had rung off, she replaced her receiver but was still staring at the telephone when Mrs. Carras came into the foyer.

"Something wrong, Miss Lewis?"

Rosemary looked up, startled, For an instant, she almost confessed, "Only that I'm feeling sorry for myself." Instead, she smiled and shook her head. "Not a thing. Don't count on me for lunch today—I'm going to walk downtown and investigate the cathedral. This is a good time for me to try some sightseeing—while the weather is good and I don't have to worry about getting wet."

The other gave a brisk nod. "They're not forecasting any more rain before evening. I'll tell Mr. Harcourt that you're downtown if he calls."

"I may go on from there," Rosemary announced, deciding that she wasn't going to be found mooning about the hotel in case Daniel came back early. "Penzance sounds interesting, too. Don't expect me till dinnertime," she added blithely over her shoulder as she started up the stairs to get her coat.

Despite her determination to enjoy the day, she discovered early on that inspecting cathedrals and shopping by herself really wasn't all it was supposed to be. Even when she boarded a train after lunch for the short journey to Penzance, she found that the town didn't have the Gilbert and Sullivan aura that she'd imagined. Annoyed with herself, she deliberately window-shopped and stopped for tea so that she wouldn't be back on the hotel doorstep too early.

Thus she was more annoyed than ever when she did arrive to find that she'd barely missed Daniel's brief stopover at the hotel. Mrs. Carras volunteered the information, but Rosemary found that he'd left a note in the middle of her bedspread as soon as she entered her small room.

"Decided it was silly for you to stay in here when you might as well have the larger quarters next door," he wrote in a distinctive script that looked as forceful as his words. "Especially since I'm going to be busy for the rest of the week. Presume that you won't object so I've moved your belongings."

Without even taking into consideration a "would you" or "if it's all right." Simply "Presume you won't object." Rosemary's lips tightened with annoyance and she strode into the other room to see her suitcase on top of the bureau and her clothes ready to hang in the armoire. Almost as they'd been the fateful night she'd arrived, except now there was no chance of being interrupted. Her expression became even more set as she realized that was the real reason she was unhappy. Certainly there was no other explanation; her new room was twice the size of her other quarters. Daniel must have decided his move was the sensible and gentlemanly thing to do.

She rubbed her forehead tiredly and picked up the room key he'd left on the bureau, putting it in her purse with an abrupt gesture. Then she marched back into her former room and left her key in the middle of the bedspread after making sure the door was unlocked.

Not that he was apt to walk in very soon. She learned that at dinner when Mrs. Carras led her to a table for one, saying that since Mr. Harcourt had taken a train for London that afternoon—he certainly wouldn't be in for dinner.

No wonder he'd changed rooms, Rosemary thought irritably. At the rate things were going, she'd be lucky to manage a formal farewell with the man before she left Cornwall. She skipped coffee in the lounge afterwards and decided on another early night—since there wasn't really any alternative. At least she knew better than to lie awake listening for signs of occupancy from next door.

Afterwards, she couldn't remember what had awakened her in the middle of the night. She had been dreaming earlier on, but had turned over and gone back to sleep once she'd retrieved her extra comforter, which had slithered onto the floor.

The next thing she heard was a metallic noise cutting into the nighttime quiet. Her eyelids flashed open as if there'd been an artillery explosion in front of the hotel, and she stared bewilderedly at the moonlight flooding the room. She frowned and was about to get up and investigate when the scraping sound was repeated. That time, she had no trouble telling it came from her hall door.

"Daniel!" she thought as her pulse rate bounded. He must have forgotten that he'd changed rooms! Then, abruptly, she remembered that he'd left his room key along with his note and he wasn't the type to forget it.

Another muffled noise at the door showed that the intruder was applying more force. By then, Rosemary was paralyzed with fright, unable even to reach for the lamp switch. It took the final clicking of the lock bolt to galvanize her into action, and her scream sounded at the exact moment the door was cautiously opened.

Her outcry froze the intruder in his tracks and then he whirled in retreat down the corridor. He must have collided with the small table, because the hotel's calm was shattered when it crashed to the floor along with the vase atop it. Rosemary's mind ticked them off even as she jumped out of bed and lunged for her robe. At that point, the bathroom door flew open so hard that it slammed against the armoire behind it.

"What in the devil's going on . . ." Daniel broke off with a painful exclamation as his toe caught the edge of the carpet. "Dammit to hell!"

It was a testimonial to Rosemary's distraught state of mind that she found nothing even remotely amusing in the fact that he was lurching about in her bedroom in the middle of the night clad only in a pair of pajama bottoms. She didn't hesitate even to fasten her robe before launching herself across the room at him. "Somebody broke in—he jimmied the lock—"

Daniel was caught off balance by her rush, barely managing to stay upright as she clutched his waist. "You're all right?" he asked tersely, as his hands fastened on her shoulders.

"Oh, yes." She swallowed and went on in a trembling voice. "When I screamed—he ran."

"Then he didn't come . . ."

Whatever else he was going to ask was overruled by a stern voice from the doorway. "Really, Mr. Harcourt. Whatever's going on?"

Daniel stiffened and pulled Rosemary around so he could face Mrs. Carras's formidable figure. In a purple tartan robe which could have doubled as a small tent, she clearly exhibited the forces of purity, right, and all the laws of the British Empire. Daniel removed Rosemary's arms from his waist, giving her derrière an absent-minded pat in the process. "Apparently there was an intruder, Mrs. Carras."

"Is that who upset the hall table?"

"Well, I certainly didn't." Rosemary pulled her robe around her and regained the offensive. "I heard someone running down the hall right after I screamed."

Daniel had taken advantage of their discussion to go back to his room, and emerged wearing a dark blue travel robe. He was still tying the belt as he started toward the hallway, saying, "Let's take a look. I doubt if we'll find anything but . . ."

"I tell you, there *was* a man," Rosemary proclaimed angrily.

"I don't doubt it," Daniel said, over his shoulder. "I just meant that he must be long gone by now."

He went out, trailed by the hotel manageress, who was declaring, "But we've never had anything like this! We've been so very careful about our clientele."

Daniel's wry voice came floating back. "I doubt if this was a registered guest. Too bad about your table. It's going to take some repair job to fix the leg."

Rosemary hovered by her door, reluctant to let them out of her sight until another blast of cold air made her retreat to the middle of her bed—the comforter pulled around her, Indian fashion.

Daniel found her in there when he returned ten minutes later, carrying a short length of pipe in his hand. He closed the door behind him and checked the lock before dropping the pipe on the bureau. "That's all we found."

"You mean 'whoever-it-was' brought it along?" Rosemary's eyes grew even wider.

"That was Mrs. Carras's reaction, too. Move over." Daniel sat down on the foot of her bed and salvaged the edge of her comforter. "It feels like the North Pole in here."

Rosemary nodded, her mind still on the more important topic. "You didn't catch a glimpse of him, then?"

"Just a broken lock on the annex door. There didn't seem any point in waking people up to ask a bunch of silly questions. Incidentally, I told Mrs. Carras that we'd changed rooms. To explain how you were on the scene."

Rosemary's cheeks took on a pink cast, despite the cold air in the bedroom. "I'll bet she didn't believe you."

"Who cares? You're missing the point, too. That intruder must have thought I was still in this room. Maybe I should thank you for saving my life."

She stared at him, trying to decide if he were serious.

As she fumbled for the right thing to say, he nodded grimly. "I'm sorry that you got caught in the middle. There's been a lot of money invested at Wheal Tamar and right now I'm a very unpopular fellow with some factions."

"But why?"

"Because I went to London this afternoon to tell the mine's board of directors that the latest exploration report on the mine's potential was cockeyed. I suspected it was misleading from the outset, and that last shaft explosion was a definite tip-off that somebody's getting desperate."

"But you still don't know who it is?"

He dropped his gaze, ostensibly to pull some more of the comforter his way. "That's the damnable part. I don't have any real proof. And the consultant they hired for the exploration report is insisting that his theory is just as valid as mine. Fortunately," Daniel added dryly, "I have a better track record."

She surveyed him and nodded slowly, not doubting in the least that his career qualifications were impressive. That much she'd learned before she ever left home. "Do you think that the tire slashing was part of the same plan?" she asked. Then, before he could say anything, she added, "And don't bring up Simon again. You'll never convince me that he knows a thing about tin mines. He was in another field altogether before he came to Cornwall. And he certainly isn't the type for slashing tires in a muddy parking lot or—" she gestured toward the bureau, "to come calling with a length of pipe."

"You're probably right. Anyhow, our intruder was smart to make a quick exit. If he'd tried to hang around these halls, he'd have frostbite or hypothermia by now." Daniel yawned mightily and swung his legs onto the floor.

"What are you—" Rosemary's voice failed her and she had to swallow before she could finish. "What are you going to do?"

"Go back to bed. Not that there's much left of the night." He yawned again and checked his watch in the dim light of the room. "We'll have to do something about your lock. The damned thing's been jimmied so it won't work." He looked around the room impatiently and went over to heft the only chair—a lightweight wood model. "I can prop this under the doorknob if it will make you feel better."

Rosemary surged to her knees although she stayed

in the middle of her bed. "It wouldn't," she said in a very decided voice.

Daniel paused to frown over his shoulder at her. "What does that mean?"

"I'd be petrified if that's all that's going to be between me and some pipe-carrying maniac."

"That's ridiculous when the pipe's right there." He gestured toward the bureau.

"I know where it is. But what's going to keep him from coming back?"

"Well, then—take my bed. The lock still works in that room," he said, jerking his head toward the smaller bedroom.

"That doesn't change anything here."

"I meant that I'd be in here," he explained patiently, "and I'm not worried."

"You should be." She bit the words off. "What if I hadn't heard that creature in the first place?"

Daniel opened his mouth to argue and then closed it again, replacing the chair against the wall as he asked resignedly, "Okay. Exactly what *did* you have in mind? I'd rather not spend the rest of the night playing gin rummy. It's too damned cold for one thing."

"I don't mean to be a nuisance. It's just that I can still see that man's shadow at the door. You go on back to bed—I probably won't close my eyes again until daylight."

"That's stupid."

"All right—so I'm stupid," she flared back at him. "I'm also not used to things like this. We may undercut our competitors in the import business but we don't take after them with a length of pipe."

He looked nonplussed for a moment and then grinned reluctantly. "I can see your point. Well, there's always the bathtub—the locks still work on the bathroom doors." When she didn't deign to reply, he added tentatively, "If it would make you feel better, I could hang around until you get to sleep."

She glanced warily around the austere bedroom, as if convincing herself that the straight chair and a dressing table bench were the only amenities where a man could sit down. Other than the obvious place, of course. Almost reluctantly her gaze went to the mattress beside her before she met his glance again.

"If you're worried about salvaging your virtue," he said wryly, "I can assure you that this is the last place I'd schedule an orgy. My God, it would be like looking for 'la dolce vita' in Newark." He started toward the other bedroom. "I'm going to get the blanket from my bed."

He was back in a minute or two with the comforter wrapped around his shoulders. Rosemary quickly moved to one side of her mattress even as she said weakly, "I feel terribly guilty. Will you be warm enough with just one blanket?"

"Are you offering yours, too?" He sat down on the other side of the bed and propped himself against the headboard, reaching across to the bed table for the paperback she'd been reading earlier.

"Not exactly." She shivered involuntarily. "We might share the wealth."

"In that case, you'll have to get considerably closer."

There was no hiding the amusement in his tone, and she felt her cheeks redden. If the room temperature hadn't been like Nome in midwinter, she would have stayed squarely where she was, but she hesitated only for a moment and then moved toward the middle of the bed.

"It's all right," he said, trying to keep his voice solemn. "I'll just stay between the blankets. We're not actually in bed together."

"Thanks very much."

"Not at all." He accomplished the maneuver, leaning across her to tuck in the blanket without a waste motion. Rosemary knew that her efforts weren't as efficient, especially when she managed to yank her sheet out at the bottom during the exchange. She seethed silently as Daniel took care of that problem, too.

"Comfortable?" he asked finally.

"Just fine," she said with a clenched jaw.

"Good. You won't mind if I read, will you?" He held up the novel he'd appropriated.

"Not at all." She chewed on her lip and wondered what to say next, finally settling for "I hope you'll be warm enough."

"No problem. Just go to sleep. And don't worry. Nobody will get in while I'm here—I promise you that."

She knew that he was doing everything in his power to reassure her and she should have been grateful. Instead, she found herself grinding her teeth as she thumped her pillow, trying to make a dent for her head. That maneuver proved ineffective, too— since the pillow was made of sturdy stuff and could have doubled as a doorstop at the hotel entrance.

"Are you all right?"

Daniel's casual question caught Rosemary still staring down at it and she wondered why she'd given even a moment's thought to the possible dangers of sharing a bed. That was the trouble with reading books on the new sexual revolution, she told herself bitterly. They listed all the maneuvers of a man on the make but the man who preferred a good mystery novel didn't rate a paragraph.

"I asked if you were all right." This time there was no hiding the irritation in his voice.

"Peachy dandy," she muttered, lying in her teeth. "If you'd ever let me get to sleep." She subsided into her pillow, pulling the blankets around her so that only the tip of her nose protruded, and filching the major portion of the covers in the process.

Almost immediately, she felt the covers yanked back. There wasn't much else that Daniel could do without tapping her on the shoulder to complain.

She waited, stiff and expectant, to see what would happen. As the minutes passed, she realized that she'd gotten away with it, unchallenged. Or ignored, which was worse.

Deliberately, she made her muscles relax as she lay on the hard mattress. Daniel had only promised to stay until she'd fallen asleep and it was a matter of feminine pride to show how efficiently she could accomplish that!

She made herself take deep, measured breaths, deciding that if she played the role well enough, he'd surmise she was already asleep and go back to his room. Then when he was out of the way, she could sit up and read for the rest of the night herself!

She was so intent on her plan that she fell sound asleep during one of her deep breathing exercises and knew nothing until considerably later.

The discreet rattle of crockery finally brought her awake, and when she'd identified the noise as morning tea her eyes went very wide indeed. A moment later, as she tried to check her travel clock, she realized a considerable weight on her chest kept her solidly anchored in the middle of the bed. She raised her head almost fearfully and discovered that somehow during the night Daniel had abandoned reading for sleeping—managing to get under the blankets while using her for a pillow. One of his arms rested possessively across her hips—so that sliding out from under him was virtually impossible.

At that moment he stirred and burrowed his head into her breasts even more comfortably. Rosemary's heartbeat rocketed under his touch and she frowned, sure that its thundering would bring him back to consciousness before she'd figured how to handle the situation.

The hotel maid bringing the early tea had no such

compunction and her knock on the hall door staved off any hope of a leisurely awakening.

As Daniel stirred, Rosemary quickly shut her eyes, hoping that he'd think she made a habit of sleeping through fire, earthquakes, and especially morning tea. It was undoubtedly a cowardly course to take but she didn't have the nerve to wish him a casual "good morning" from her position.

Although she kept her eyelids tightly shut, there wasn't anything wrong with her hearing and she didn't miss Daniel's swift, indrawn breath when he realized where his head was resting. Nor was there any disguising his pithy, muttered reaction. He must have subjected her sleeping face to a thorough examination then, because several seconds elapsed before he slid carefully away from her. Even so, Rosemary wondered if he would have made the move if there hadn't been a frustrated rattle of the doorknob after the chair wedge held firm.

"I'll leave your tea out here, Mr. Harcourt," the waitress announced when she couldn't do anything else.

Daniel's next mutter told what he thought of the whole institution of morning tea and made Rosemary decide to wake up. It was one thing to ignore sharing her bed but she'd have to have been drugged or unconscious to sleep through such a commotion.

She stretched and slowly opened her eyes. Unfortunately, she looked right into Daniel's sardonic gaze as he came back to the bed carrying two cups of tea.

Rosemary shoved her hair back and sat up, saying brightly, "Is it *that* time already?"

Daniel banged the cups down on the bedside table so hard that the tea sloshed into the saucers. "It's a hell of a lot later than I thought. I have to get out of here."

"But what about your tea?"

"I don't want the damned stuff. You drink it," he said, tightening the belt on his robe as he headed toward the bathroom.

"Daniel . . ."

Her voice caught him halfway and he paused with one hand on the door jamb. "What is it?"

"Did you manage to get any sleep?" she asked, wondering how much he would admit.

His eyes narrowed as he surveyed her figure upright in the middle of the blankets. "Enough," he said finally. "Why?"

"No reason," she replied, matching his evasion. "Do you want to take the book with you?" When he frowned at her, she said, "So you can finish the story."

"I think the management at Wheal Tamar would prefer that I did some mapping instead," he drawled. "Thanks just the same."

"You mean you're going down that shaft again today?"

"It happens to be my job. If I still have one when I finally get out of here."

He closed the bathroom door sharply on that and a

moment later Rosemary heard the shower turned on full force.

If he had any regret about leaving his warm bed, he'd certainly managed to hide it, she decided, and reached for one of the cups of tea.

She remained in the bundle of blankets while she drank it, not thrilled at being found in that position when Daniel finally left for work but not wanting to scramble into her clothes without at least washing her face. Then she remembered the public bathroom down the hallway and hopped out of bed, pulling on her robe to gather her clothes.

Fortunately, the public bathroom was untenanted and she was able to bathe and dress in relative comfort. She put on a plaid skirt and pale yellow cashmere sweater, thinking that with a dark gray blazer they'd be appropriate for her appointment with Claire and later for lunch with Simon. As she zipped her cosmetic bag and prepared to go back to the bedroom, she wondered what Daniel's reaction would be to that luncheon date.

She needn't have worried about confronting him with the information. As soon as she entered the room and saw the open bathroom door she knew that she'd missed him again.

Mrs. Carras confirmed it as she came down the hallway with a tray to retrieve the teacups. "Mr. Harcourt never stops running, does he? Poor man—he certainly earns his salary."

"Maybe I can still catch up with him in the dining room," Rosemary said, as if it didn't matter one way or the other.

"He didn't wait for breakfast. That blonde came to pick him up again. He said something to her about stopping for coffee on the way."

"I see." Rosemary managed to sound casual as she tossed her cosmetic bag into her suitcase.

"I'm terribly sorry that you were bothered last night—"

Rosemary, thinking of Daniel, said defensively, "But I wasn't. Absolutely nothing happened. Not a thing."

The older woman frowned from the threshold. "Well, heaven knows what *would* have happened if you hadn't screamed."

"I just meant that it could have been worse," Rosemary stammered.

"It was bad enough—he ruined the table in the hall as well as this lock. I promised Mr. Harcourt to have it replaced today for sure." Mrs. Carras jerked her head toward the length of pipe still atop the bureau. "We're changing the lock on the annex door, too. Just in case 'whoever-it-was' plans to come back. You'll be down for breakfast, won't you?"

Rosemary, whose appetite had dwindled, nodded.

"You'll feel better after coffee," the older woman added in a comforting tone and headed for the stairs with her tray.

Rosemary watched her go and then walked over to stare out of the window into another morning made somber with gathering clouds. The scene almost appeared to be a forerunner of events and she doubted if anything as simple as coffee would make very much difference in the outcome.

Chapter Six

By the time ten o'clock rolled around, Rosemary had taken herself firmly in hand. What she needed to do was secure her job order with Claire Rome and keep unimportant things—like Daniel's actions—firmly at the back of her mind.

When Simon drove up in his car, she was waiting by the hotel porch, scuffing her shoe aimlessly in the pile of still-sodden leaves by the bottom of the steps.

Simon flashed his bright grin as he got out. "Good morning. Are all American women so prompt or am I just lucky?"

There was no answer to that so she merely smiled and said, "It's awfully nice of you to play chauffeur. I think I'm the lucky one." She hesitated before getting into the car, casting a dubious glance at the overcast sky. "Do you think I should take a raincoat?"

He appeared to consider it and then shook his head. "No need. I have one on the back seat that we can share if it's raining by the time we get to

Mousehole. There's a car park close to the restaurant so we shouldn't get very wet."

"We are going to see your sister first, aren't we?"

He nodded and helped her in the car. "I'd finish up as a dustman if I didn't take you by the house. Claire was putting on coffee for us when I left."

Rosemary waited until he was behind the wheel and had started the car to ask, "Is she feeling better today?"

"Absolutely tickety-boo." He grinned again, seeing her puzzled expression as he pulled out onto the street in front of the hotel. "Sorry, I keep forgetting that you're a foreigner. Claire's just fine. A bit intense over this doll business but you can understand that."

Rosemary nodded, deciding that Claire Rome was fortunate to have a brother who advised her on her career and was close enough to help when other troubles threatened. She shot a covert glance his way, thinking that the tall, fair-haired man at her side was the intense type, too, despite his determinedly casual air. There was no denying his wiry good looks, especially in his dark green sports jacket with gray wool slacks.

Simon was going on. "I've told her that this doll scheme isn't worth the headaches, unless she can develop a lucrative outlet in the States." He turned and winked before pulling onto the highway that skirted Truro. "That's why I'm engineering today's lend-lease act."

"You mean, I'm to be wined and dined on the expense account?" Rosemary kept her tone solemn.

"That's it, pet. I certainly won't tell Claire that I'd already mentioned this lunch when we met on the train."

"I'm looking forward tremendously to seeing Mousehole," Rosemary told him, thinking it would do no harm to change the subject.

"I knew it. All the Americans head for there if they have a few hours spare. Fortunately, there is a good place to eat."

"Cornish pasties?"

He grinned at her wry tone. "I can tell you've hit a clanger already. Would you settle for a delicious crab sandwich?"

"In a flash!" Rosemary was thinking how she'd manage to mention her delightful lunch the next time she saw Daniel. That fleeting thought brought her to another, more sober, topic. "Will your brother-in-law be home this morning?"

"Edwin? He was there earlier—watching a rerun of the snooker competition on the telly—but I think he left right after I did."

It was on the tip of Rosemary's tongue to ask what a snooker competition was. Surely they played it on a pool table—or was it a billiard table? She mentally threw in the towel at that point, deciding there were some things beyond transatlantic comprehension. "I gather that you and he don't have much to do with the actual running of Claire's business," she said finally.

"Not unless we're dragged into it. I can remember spending one entire Sunday stuffing arms and legs of the little blighters, and that was enough for me."

"At least Claire didn't ask you to sew hems on the dresses."

"Am I supposed to be grateful for that?"

"Sorry." She pursed her lips thoughtfully. "I imagine that finding a dependable labor force is one of the biggest problems for cottage industry."

"You're right about that, and getting buyers to pay their bills is another one. Present company excepted, of course."

"Of course," she agreed as he slowed to turn into the quiet residential street she remembered. Rosemary noticed that the Romes' lawn hadn't been cut in the interval and the front gate was still listing on its hinges. Apparently Claire's husband didn't spend his time on such menial tasks, and she doubted if Simon was the type to volunteer, either.

"You *are* coming in, aren't you?"

Simon's puzzled query finally penetrated and she discovered that while she was daydreaming, he'd parked and was holding the car door for her.

"Sorry, I was woolgathering." She got out beside him on the parking strip, waving to his sister when she opened the front door and smiled at them.

A minute later, Claire greeted them in cheerful if slightly distraught fashion as they came up the front steps. "I shouldn't let anybody in this house," she confessed. "It looks as if a gale had hit it."

"It usually does," Simon said drily, following the two women into the small front hallway. "Fortunately, you have other talents to make up for being generally messy."

"That sounds exactly like something my family would say," Rosemary cut in before Claire could reply. "I never take any notice. Besides, it's hard when you have to work at home."

"I've certainly found that out." Claire gestured ahead of her. "Come on, we might as well go back to the extra bedroom. I have most of my samples in there."

Simon hung back. "I'll bring the coffee in and then have mine in the kitchen while you two conduct your business."

"I don't mind your sticking around," Rosemary started to say, only to have him cut in.

"Actually, I have some phone calls I should make. It's better this way. Black coffee or white?"

"Black, thanks." He disappeared into a kitchen archway as she followed Claire down the short hallway to another open door. On the way, she glimpsed a tiny room crowded with furniture where a television console took up most of one wall. There was a pungent smell of cigar smoke, which changed to cigarette smoke as she entered the small bedroom where Claire awaited her. An inexpensive student desk piled high with papers was next to the single bed piled equally high with doll clothes. Two shelves along the other wall were crammed with different versions of a medium-sized rag doll. The same red cheeks, bright blue eyes, and wide smile appeared on the faces but there were several hair styles—the wigs ranging from tight black curls to a blonde Dutch bob.

The outfits varied widely, too, from calico dresses and shawls to corduroy pants with matching jacket tops. One doll featured a dark blue sailor suit with a perky white hat, while the one next to her wore an ankle-length gauzy gown and had a miniature feather boa around her shoulders.

Simon appeared in the doorway bearing the mugs of coffee and handed them over. "I'll leave you two in peace."

Claire smiled her thanks. "Proper job, my handsome."

He waved airily and disappeared to make his phone calls.

Rosemary took her gaze from the doll display long enough to say, "He's very proud of what you've done. I can tell."

Claire flushed with pleasure and took a quick sip of her coffee to hide her embarrassment. "That's enough about us. How do you like my babies?"

"They're charming. There's a tremendous originality in the expressions and a lot of thought went into the costuming. Who's your main designer?" As Claire looked even more embarrassed, Rosemary said, "Good heavens! You really *are* the moving force! I thought you mainly pulled the operation together."

"That, too. Only it's not together in the way I'd prefer. The lady who's been doing the dresses has a

Mum who's just been sent to hospital," Claire said, ticking off one finger. "My arm-and-leg stuffer can't be depended on and that means that I've been hauled in to finish those. What are you smiling about?"

"Simon was telling me about the time he stuffed arms and legs. He wasn't enchanted with the job."

"That's putting it mildly, and my husband's even worse when I have to call on him. I'd have given up the project before this except that it's been so well received by my customers. Actually getting orders is the least troublesome part of the operation. We can't be as competitive on price as the Far Eastern imports but doll collectors don't seem to mind."

"The trouble is—my boss is adamant about a firm delivery date. How many dolls do you have available at the moment?"

The figure Claire named made Rosemary frown and chew on her thumbnail, since it wasn't nearly the quantity she'd hoped to air-freight before she left London.

"I know," Claire said when the silence lengthened. "The business is at a bad patch right now and there's no use pretending anything different."

"Can you recruit some more people to help you?"

"There *are* some members of a church guild at St. Ives who make stuffed toys as a project. I've been planning to find out if they'd want to earn a bit extra. How soon do you have to know?"

"Within the next day or two," Rosemary said ruefully. "I'd planned on flying home next week and

I'll have to check out some other possibilities if you can't manage the numbers I need."

Claire's concern was evident, but she nodded. "I understand. I'll try to contact the guild president today."

"And your husband?"

The other's head snapped around at Rosemary's question. "What about him?"

"Why, nothing. I mean nothing special. It's just that I thought you'd want to check with him before you committed your firm to a big overseas order. I know that it can cause problems when a wife is working."

"That's what I've been trying to tell my sister," Simon said, materializing suddenly in the doorway. "Frankly, I think she'd do better to leave things to the men of the family."

"Well, I don't happen to agree with you," Claire said, slamming her coffee mug onto the already crowded desk top. "And I refuse to give up a growing business just because you and Edwin have other ideas."

Simon threw up his hands as he turned to glance at Rosemary. "You can tell this is a familiar refrain."

"I'm sorry," Claire said, showing her chagrin at involving a stranger in their family fight. "Simon and I can discuss this later. Tell me, where are you two going for lunch?"

"A restaurant in Mousehole," Rosemary said, visibly relieved by her change of subject. "Simon's humoring me; I was bound and determined to visit the place while I was in Cornwall—ever since I looked at a map of England. I have to be convinced that it's a real town and not something out of Lewis Carroll."

"Actually it *does* look a little bit like a fairy tale," Simon said, folding his arms over his chest as he leaned against the door frame. "You'll find the fishermen are real, though. And even though they don't admit it—I have the feeling that the setting fascinates them, too."

"All that and a good restaurant, besides," Claire said, perching atop some of the papers on the end of the desk. "I envy you."

"Why don't you come along?" Rosemary coaxed impulsively. "We'd love to have you."

Claire bubbled with laughter as she glanced at her brother. "Oh, Simon! If you could only see your expression! Don't worry—I won't play gooseberry." She turned back to Rosemary. "But it was sweet of you to suggest it."

"I meant it."

"I know—and I'd love to take the time off, but I have to talk to that church guild. A friend of mine who paints the dolls' faces is going to pick me up. She needs the extra income, too."

"I won't insist then," Rosemary said, smiling in sympathy. "Since I'm the one who's cracking the whip, I can't very well lead you astray."

"Thank the Lord for that," Simon breathed fervently. He went over to put an arm about Claire's shoulders and give her a brief hug, "Not that I don't love you, but . . ."

". . . two's company and three's still a crowd," she finished, moving away determinedly. "Now you'd better get going or you'll have to wait forever."

"I've made a reservation," Simon told her.

"So did some friends of ours—and they still had to wait an hour when they went to dinner there last week."

"All right. I'm convinced." Simon gestured Rosemary toward the door.

She nodded and gave him her coffee mug, watching him deposit it beside a doll on the shelf before she turned back to Claire. "I hate to go off with everything still up in the air. I'd hoped to have everything neatly finished by now."

"There's nothing I would have liked better," the other said, trailing them into the hallway.

"Unfortunately, that's one of the hazards of cottage industry," Simon cut in. "Rough edges have to be expected. Maybe Claire can still pull it together."

His sister opened the front door for them, saying as she leaned back against it, "I'll do everything I can. There's too much at stake to let my company slip away at this point."

"That's all very well, but you have to keep things in perspective," Simon insisted. "It won't help if you're a silly twit and find yourself back on the invalid list. Edwin deserves better from a wife."

Claire winced visibly at his criticism, but she said, "I'll be careful. There's nothing wrong with my memory, Simon."

Rosemary would have liked to vanish and reappear

at the curbside. Instead she had to ignore all the in-
nuendos and remain discreetly silent during their
family fracas.

"I'm glad you're all right," Simon was going on
to Claire, "but after taking a bump on the head,
there's always the chance of a relapse."

Was he warning Claire that her husband might
cause further harm, Rosemary wondered. If so, why
on earth couldn't he put the fear of God into Edwin
instead of frightening a woman who had more than
enough problems already? She started to say something to that effect, when Claire turned a brimming
glance her way and managed a smile.

"Poor Rosemary," she said. "You're going to think
we're all soppy in Cornwall. Take no notice of us.
I'll phone you tomorrow and let you know what
luck I've had with the church guild. And make sure
that Simon buys you an expensive lunch. He can afford it." She nodded a casual farewell and went back
in the house, closing the door behind her.

Rosemary didn't break the silence until Simon had
made a U-turn in the street and they were well on
their way to rejoining the main road. "I think your
sister's a charming person."

"Charming but not very practical. She's spread
way too thin with all that's going on and she hasn't
the physical stamina for it. But you can see what
luck I have convincing her."

"Can't her husband help out?"

"Edwin?" Simon's smile didn't have any humor in
it. "He objected to Claire's messing about with

the doll business in the first place. The only way he'd help would be to give her a firm shove and try to get her out of it altogether."

"I thought he already had," Rosemary murmured without thinking.

"What's that?"

She swallowed, trying to cover her gaffe. "I meant that his opinion was important to her," she hurried on. "I wish we'd insisted that she come with us. It's a lovely day to play hooky."

"Rather more cloud than I'd choose," he replied with a frowning glance up at the sky.

"You know what I mean." Happy to have diverted him from the Romes, she stuck to the safer topic. "Tell me, do we see anything interesting on our drive to Mousehole? I was at Penzance yesterday but that's about all."

"I thought you'd seen Tintagel. With your chum Harcourt . . ."

"Oh, I have. I'm talking about the south coast," Rosemary said, carefully avoiding his reference to Daniel. "It's surprising how much milder the temperature is once you're away from the Atlantic. I understand there are even palm trees on the Channel side of Cornwall."

"It's much milder but it can still be a ship's graveyard when the wind blows. We don't have to worry about it today. The harbor at Mousehole should be calm while we're there. Something tells me that it's the calm before another storm though," he added with a concerned look at the overcast sky.

Rosemary forgot all about his pessimism when they drove down the narrow, winding road into the storybook village just after noon. They twisted and turned, finally emerging into a town square between neat stone houses which in turn faced one of the prettiest pocket-sized harbors she'd ever seen.

A rock breakwater rimmed most of the area to ensure a quiet harborage. Just then it was partially filled with small fishing dinghies bobbing lazily at their buoys. There were nets draped on some of the dinghies and on parts of the breakwater, too. Some fishermen who were obviously enjoying the rare sunshine were adding to the collection as they watched.

"Why don't you get out here and wait while I park the car? It shouldn't take me long," Simon said, pulling to a stop at the end of the square.

Rosemary got out quickly and saw him drive away, turning out of sight around a sharp corner before he'd gone any distance at all. That wasn't surprising, she decided, as she stared around her. Everything in Mousehole seemed as Lilliputian as the town's name suggested. She almost expected small citizens to man the boats and gave a start of surprise when a toddler burst around the corner at that moment. Then she smiled in relief as the child's father—a husky six-footer—ran after the truant, swinging him up to his shoulder and making the youngster crow with happiness.

Rosemary wandered past some of the stone houses, lingering to view the display window of a tiny food shop and then walking across the cobbled street to peer over the low stone wall which was part of the sea barrier. The small fishing boats curtsied gently in the harbor currents, but there was a great deal of formidable Channel and rocky coastline beyond the Mousehole boundaries. It was easy to understand Simon's comment about its being a ship's graveyard if the weather turned nasty. Everything about Cornwall was accompanied by ominous undertones, she thought, and felt her flesh crawl as she stared out at the gray swells.

"Why, you're shivering! You should have gone into the restaurant to wait," Simon said, striding up beside her.

"You didn't tell me where we're eating. Not that it matters," she added hastily. "I'm not really cold at all. This is a charming place!"

"All the tourists like it. Let's hope that the townspeople don't get too quaint with their ideas. A little 'arty-crafty' goes a long way as far as I'm concerned. At least the place where we're eating concentrates on food as well as atmosphere." He was leading her past some of the squat, square houses to a modest stone building with mullioned windows which overlooked the harbor. Flower boxes alongside the entrance still had a few plants in bloom despite the recent storms.

A bell tinkled as Simon pushed open the restaurant door, and a dark-haired young woman behind a reception desk got to her feet. "Did you come for lunch?" she inquired politely.

"That's right. I have a reservation—the name's Hardy."

"Yes, of course." She ticked it off on her reservation list and came out from behind the counter. "Would you like the dining room or the bar?"

Rosemary had been surveying the tiny quarters with interest, amused by a beamed ceiling which was almost overpowering in the matchbox-sized room, as well as the turkey-red carpet which went down three steps to a lower level and up another steep stairway to the restaurant beyond. The red-flocked wallpaper was equally hard to ignore, and a tremendous dried flower arrangement under glass near the stairway must have come straight from somebody's attic. At any moment, she expected a parlormaid dressed in ankle-length bombazine to come tripping down the stairs.

Instead, a girl in a miniskirt dashed halfway down, saying, "There's a window seat available," to the hostess before hurrying away.

"That sounds good," Simon murmured, looking at Rosemary for confirmation.

"Fine with me . . ."

"Actually, it's in the bar," the hostess told them, "but we serve sandwiches as well as drinks up there."

"Better and better," Rosemary said, and Simon nodded his agreement.

"This way, then," the hostess said, making for the stairs. "Watch your step. It's a bit steep."

"I know how she keeps her figure," Rosemary told Simon afterwards, when they'd been directed to a bay window where there were two chintz-covered chairs with a low table between them. "If I had to climb those steps all the time—I wouldn't have to worry about my waistline either."

He pretended to inspect her carefully. "Speaking as an impartial observer, there doesn't appear to be a thing wrong with your waistline. Or any of the other vital parts."

"You know the saying—'Indulge and bulge.' And this lunch isn't going to help at all."

"I can recommend the crab sandwiches."

"They sound marvelous." She smiled and relinquished her menu to the miniskirted waitress who came to take their order.

"What about a drink to start?" Simon asked

Rosemary shook her head. "It's too early for me. Tomato juice would be nice, though."

"One tomato juice and a whisky and soda. Coffee later?" he asked Rosemary.

"Yes, thanks."

"Coffee later," he confirmed, and handed his menu to the girl.

"This is a lovely view," Rosemary said when they were alone again and she'd turned the chair so she could see the entire length of the harbor. "There's something completely unreal about this part of the world. If I couldn't see those two freighters in the Channel, I'd swear we'd gone back a hundred years in time." She gestured toward two old men sitting atop the tide-washed rocks on the breakwater, "Even those fishermen might have stepped right off a Victorian stage."

Simon leaned forward to see where she was looking and said cynically, "Their clothes probably did."

"You don't sound as if this is—" she broke off and started to giggle.

"What's so funny?"

"Sorry. I was going to say 'your cup of tea' and then I realized how silly it sounded."

"I must admit that I prefer the London scene. That's another place where Claire and I differ."

Rosemary stifled a sigh. Apparently he was determined to lead the conversation back to his favorite topic. It would serve him right if she countered with a dissertation on how the British weather had wrecked her sinuses or some other ghoulish and imaginary problem. Not for anything would she have revealed that she'd spent most of the drive to Mousehole wondering how Daniel was faring—and if he were reliving the way they'd spent the night as she was—despite her efforts to the contrary.

The waitress arrived with their drinks at that moment. She served the juice and Simon's scotch, while announcing, "The sandwiches should be ready soon."

"Good! I'm starved," Simon said and picked up his drink. "Sorry you wouldn't join me," he told Rosemary as she reached for her tomato juice.

"Blame it on my single-track mind. Right now, I plan to concentrate on the crab sandwich," she told him, determined to steer their lunch conversation into a cheerful vein. On the way home, she'd stay in her tourist's role and keep him talking about local wonders. "Tell me more about this place," she went on determinedly.

"It's part hotel and part restaurant," he replied, misunderstanding her meaning. "Since the renovation, it's gained quite a reputation." A smile hovered about his lips as he replaced his drink on the table. "I hate to spoil your fantasy but I should admit that the owner hails from Los Angeles."

Rosemary looked surprised and then started to laugh. "Nothing's sacred any more."

"Not here it isn't. Frankly, the food's much better since the new management took charge."

"It would be fun to spend some time here," Rosemary said wistfully.

"Certainly more of a treat than your hotel in Truro. But maybe you haven't had time to miss the tourist amenities."

"What do you mean by that?"

"Well, I'd say Harcourt was doing his best to keep you occupied."

Rosemary swirled her tomato juice carefully in the glass. "That *could* have the earmarks of a nasty crack."

"Sorry, love." Simon reached over and patted her hand. "I didn't mean it that way. He's a nice-looking bloke—I can't blame you for wanting to bring him into the fold. And from the way he acted at Claire's—I gather he feels the same about you."

For an instant, Rosemary believed him and her heartbeat broke into a gallop until common sense prevailed. Would any man who was crazy about a woman leap out of a warm, shared bed as if the fiends of hell were after him—the way that Daniel had exited that morning? Hardly. Simon didn't know what he was talking about.

"Things are not always what they seem," she told him lightly and breathed a sigh of relief, as their lunch arrived just then.

As delicious as the crab sandwiches proved to be, Simon refused to be diverted from his favorite topic. "Does that mean that Harcourt won't be going back to London this week when you do?"

"I wouldn't put any money on it." She took another bite of sandwich, wondering if the restaurant roof would collapse if she ordered her coffee before the meal was finished.

"I'm surprised that Harcourt is so closemouthed about his work," Simon said, continuing to probe. "He's acting more like an Englishman than an American, or maybe I've been reading the wrong books about your country."

"It's a masculine trait found world-wide," Rosemary announced with some bitterness. "Adam probably dreamed up that motto about 'Never explain and never complain' in the Garden of Eden. Men always ignore the last part . . ."

". . . while remaining staunch advocates of the first!" Simon burst into laughter. "You sound exactly like Claire when she's taking after Edwin. I'll have to tell him."

"Do that." Then Rosemary shook her head ruefully. "Sorry, I'm not usually so dogmatic. I don't think I had enough sleep last night."

Simon was instantly remorseful. "I'm sorry to hear it. Nothing serious, I hope."

She almost mentioned the hotel intruder and all the subsequent furor before deciding against it. If Simon learned that she and Daniel had adjoining rooms, the conversation could take an embarrassing turn. Lord knows what he'd think if she told how she'd spent the rest of the night. Certainly he'd never believe the truth—no one in his right mind would.

"What's the matter? Something wrong with your sandwich?" he asked, puzzled.

She stared at him. "No, why?"

"You looked as if you'd bitten on a piece of shell or found some grit."

"No—it's fine." She took a deep breath and said, "Do you suppose we could have coffee now?"

"I don't see why not," he said as he peered around the chair, trying to see if a waitress were nearby. "Since the owner's a Californian, it shouldn't be difficult."

"I'm not sure about that. Southern Californians have their own life styles. Maybe he's into nuts and seeds—with no caffeine allowed on the premises."

Simon grinned but turned back to catch the eye of a passing waitress and mouthed the request for coffee across the room. When she nodded and went to get it, he sat back in the chair. "Health addicts wouldn't be serving whisky."

Rosemary smiled. "Go to the head of the class."

"There's not much I miss," he said levelly. "In Cornwall, it's best to know which way the wind blows. Safer, too, for that matter."

A slight frown creased Rosemary's forehead. If she didn't know better, there could have been an ominous undertone to his quiet comment. She gave a murmur of relief when their waitress appeared with a tray of coffee things. A hot drink might make her think more clearly and just then she needed all the help she could get.

By the time they'd finished lunch and were walking back to the car, she felt considerably more refreshed. "Thanks for bringing me here," she said to Simon at her side. "I'll remember the charm of Mousehole for a long, long time."

"My pleasure. You're the perfect woman to invite to lunch. Imagine not having to pay—just because that proprietor learned you were from the States! Are all Americans so generous?"

"Only when they're a little homesick. Don't forget, he also said he liked Cornwall air better than Los Angeles smog, so it all evened out."

He took out his keys to unlock her door as they approached the small car park. "The least I can do is take you to where the air is even fresher. How about a side trip to Land's End before we go home? I think we can just about make it before the rain starts."

"I'd like that if you're sure that it won't interfere with your plans."

"My only plans right now involve keeping the

most beautiful visitor to Cornwall with me as long as possible."

"Well, this visitor would be delighted," she said lightly and slid into the car before he could get other ideas.

Their detour to Land's End at the very tip of the Cornish peninsula wasn't far. On the way, they passed a turn-off to the popular Minack Open-Air Theatre above Porthcurno Beach.

"Too bad we haven't time to inspect that, too," Simon said, slowing his speed as he thought about it. "Most visitors take in one of their productions during the summer season."

"I'm afraid that it's either the theatre or Land's End today from the looks of the sky. I'd say another storm is brewing."

"I know." He pressed on the accelerator again. "And Land's End should get our nod."

"What is the Minack Theatre really like?" she asked, still curious on that score.

"Most people around here think it's smashing. Of course, the big thing is the setting. It's literally carved out of the hillside, so if you don't like the acting you can enjoy a tremendous view of the Channel. Of course, it can be rugged watching when the wind is blowing up a storm around you. It adds to the staging effects in a way that Shakespeare never planned."

"Why didn't somebody tell me that Cornwall was full of fascinating things—I wouldn't have spent so much time in London."

"There's always another day." Simon made a left turn on to a narrow two-lane road with a cluster of buildings at the end of it. "Anyhow, you'll get to see Land's End for sure. If you want to throw any bottles into the briny, the next stop's New York—give or take a few miles for currents on the way."

Rosemary smiled and leaned forward to note the usual collection of tour buses parked near a building which advertised souvenirs and refreshments. There wasn't any attempt at landscaping on the rocky soil; rough patches of turf grew in haphazard fashion, giving an unfinished look to the settlement despite the tourist attractions.

Simon pulled up and parked near a place which was advertised as *the first and last house*. "Want to get out or just stay in the car?"

"The least I can do is go look over the edge of the cliff." She paused with her fingers still on the door handle. "If you're sure we have time for this."

He opened his own door, saying, "Why not? I'll come with you."

They made their way down a narrow path, skirting the edge of the car park. A flock of small gray birds, searching for food in the rough turf, exploded into flight as they approached, and Rosemary lingered to watch them soar overhead. Then her attention focussed on the gray clouds rolling in from the Atlantic and she hurried to catch up with Simon.

"Want a 'cuppa'?" he asked, jerking his head toward one of the buildings which advertised refreshments.

"No, thanks—I'm just here for the view."

She stepped aside as a small group of Japanese tourists surged back toward their bus, the men busy putting their cameras safely in their cases while the women compared souvenirs they'd bought.

Rosemary pulled up as she and Simon reached a barrier at the edge of the cliff. She gestured toward the water surging against the rugged rockfaces below. "I'd hate to try and row ashore."

"You'd have quite a climb if you did make it. This is a sixty-foot granite cliff."

She nodded, taking a deep breath of the biting but refreshing salt air. "I'm getting used to your cliffs. There isn't a soft edge in all of Cornwall."

"Just soft rain," Simon judged, holding out his palm to make sure.

Rosemary fished in her jacket pocket for a scarf, which she tied over her hair as they turned back toward the car. "At least we timed it right. You must own a crystal ball."

"Well, right now it's telling me not to waste time," he said, quickening the pace. "From the way that wind is blowing, we'd best be off."

Rosemary was breathless when they got back in the car. "Five minutes later and we'd have needed raincoats for sure."

"Did you get very wet?" Simon wanted to know, pulling a clean white handkerchief from his pocket and offering it to her.

"Just a little damp in spots. That's better, thanks,"

she said as she handed it back to him after patting her face dry.

He shoved the handkerchief into his pocket and turned on the ignition. "We can use the heater to finish. It should be warm soon."

The trip back to Truro was taken in a contented silence, after that. Raindrops on the windshield and the occasional buffeting of the wind made the interior of the car seem a cozy haven against the weather outside. The feeling intensified as the thick gray clouds filled in every vacant bit of space overhead, changing the late afternoon into dusky twilight.

Rosemary was grateful to Simon for driving carefully on the two-lane road, which often had only narrow shoulders or none at all. That drawback was coupled with a network of side roads, dangerously hidden behind hedgerows or stone fences. The trip would have been a challenge under the best of conditions; in the dusk and rain it presented untold hazards to a driver.

It apparently took its toll on Simon, because he let out an audible sigh of relief as they finally pulled into the brightly lit forecourt of the Carras Hotel, bringing the car to a stop directly in front of the porch steps. "I can't park here long but you won't get very wet before you're under cover. Or you can borrow my mac—I'll retrieve it another time."

He would have reached into the back of the car for the raincoat but Rosemary put a restraining hand on his arm. "I don't need it, thanks. It's been a wonderful day, Simon," she went on when he settled back behind the wheel. "Lunch was fantastic and I enjoyed our sightseeing, too. I only hope that Claire was as fortunate."

"Who knows? I try not to get mixed up in Claire's dealings—it's easier that way. Edwin paid for the privilege but brothers are allowed to watch from the sidelines."

"I had the idea you were very close—" Rosemary broke off then, apologetic. "Sorry, I didn't mean to sound so nosy. At any rate, I'll call her tomorrow."

"Fair enough." He shifted in the seat to face her. "You're sure that you're in good shape? Not damp or chilled?"

"No, of course not. Why? What makes you think so?"

"I didn't want to take unfair advantage of you," he informed her with a grin as he put his hands on her shoulders and pulled her gently but firmly toward him. "An old British custom . . ." he murmured just before his mouth came down on hers.

His tongue coaxed and beguiled in the interval that followed, trying to change the kiss from a chaste farewell to something considerably different. Rosemary kept her own lips together despite his maneuvering, and when his hands shifted under the front of her jacket, she pushed back quickly. "That's enough."

He sighed audibly. "I could fancy you, Rosemary, love. Do you really have to go in?"

The plaintive request caught Rosemary as much

by surprise as his unexpectedly passionate leavetaking. "I really do," she lied gamely, surprised that Simon was making his romantic overtures in front of the hotel rather than when they'd roamed picturesque Mousehole or stopped to admire parts of Cornwall's south coast. She attempted to smooth her hair before reaching for her door handle. "It's getting late . . ."

"I know the drill," he cut in. "It just seems such a bloody waste! I *will* see you before you go back to London, won't I?"

Rosemary tried to hide her annoyance, knowing there was no reason to be rude just because he'd made a pass at her. "Probably. If you're around Claire's house. I'm hoping to place a firm order with her in the next day or so. Those dolls may be a pain in the neck to you but they're money in the bank to my boss. He's sure they'll sell."

"Let's skip any more mention of business tactics. Mind you, I could use them as an excuse."

Rosemary couldn't help but respond. "You win— we'll take things as they come. Thank you again for today. Now—stay here—there's no reason for you to get soaked." She pushed open her car door and got out into the stormy darkness, hesitating just long enough to slam the door behind her before dashing toward the lighted hotel entrance. Her head was down but she heard Simon gun his engine and roar off toward the street.

An instant later, she was under cover, pulling up at the glass doors to catch her breath and colliding with a solid object in the process. "Oh, I'm terribly sorry," she said, wiping the rain from her eyes. "I didn't see you—oh, lord!"

"So I gathered," Daniel said tersely when her voice trailed off at discovering her victim. "I'd hate to think you staged that performance in the car just for my benefit."

"I don't know what . . ." she began and then changed her tone in mid-sentence as his meaning penetrated. "You can't really think I'd do anything so childish."

"I haven't seen any particular symptoms of your mature mind so far—but something could have passed me by."

"I doubt it," she flared back. "Nothing would dare escape that damned eagle-eye of yours! Don't you have more to do than spy on people?"

"What the hell makes you think I was spying?"

"Evidently you were hanging around . . ."

"I happened to get here just before Hardy pulled up."

"Some people would have gone on into the lounge instead of being a . . . a . . . nosey-parker," she retorted, wishing that she could have found a more withering description to deflate him.

"It wasn't your drawn-out necking session that kept me here," he informed her with distaste. "I needed to get something from the trunk of my car and I didn't want the two of you as an audience. Besides, you were in the way."

Her chin went up. "A position I seem to have occupied ever since I've arrived."

"You said it. I didn't," he retorted silkily. "Now, if you'll excuse me . . ."

As he turned up the collar of his jacket and started down the steps toward the parking area, Rosemary had an insane desire to administer a firm push right in the middle of those formidable shoulders and send him sprawling. She kept her hands clenched at her sides with an effort, but the epithet that she muttered as she went inside must have carried further than she thought, because Mrs. Carras, who was emerging from the lounge, gave her a startled look.

"I beg your pardon!" the hotel woman said, drawing herself up as far as her well-corseted girth allowed.

"I was talking about this ghastly weather!" Rosemary said quickly as she brushed the rain from the front of her jacket. "Honestly, it's more like December than September. I didn't dream there'd be so many storms at this time of year."

"There's no accounting for it," Mrs. Carras agreed, deciding that she must have misunderstood Rosemary's American accent. "It's a good thing that we don't depend on the tourist trade like some other hotels. Most of our guests are businessmen or people who've come to visit relatives." She moved toward the dining room and then paused in the archway. "Will you and Mr. Harcourt be wanting dinner?"

Rosemary had started up the stairs but she lingered

on the second step. "I will. I have no idea of Mr. Harcourt's plans."

Mrs. Carras's eyebrows rose at the cool response. "I see. Well, he'll probably tell me. Oh, I knew there was something else!" She went back to the reception counter and emerged with a key, which she handed to Rosemary. "I had the lock changed on room three today along with the one on the annex door."

"Thank you. That was quick work."

The manageress nodded. "Let's hope it solves the problem. I hate to think of such people in Truro. It's still a shock to read about the goings-on in London or Liverpool."

And even more disconcerting when it happens to you, Rosemary felt like saying as she went on up the stairs and unlocked her door.

By then, she'd simmered down slightly after her encounter with Daniel. Enough so that she peeked over the stair railing to see if he'd come back into the hotel before she went into her room.

Daniel's disdainful attitude made her realize that she'd have her work cut out convincing him of what really happened during Simon's leavetaking. She stared unhappily toward the other room, thinking that maybe he wouldn't even come back to hear any explanations. Certainly he hadn't shown the slightest disposition to linger—just the opposite, in fact.

The sharp frown on Rosemary's forehead deepened an instant later when there came a thud on her hall door. She took a step toward it and then called apprehensively, "Who is it?"

"Parker. As in Nosey. Unlock the door, will you!"

Rosemary's frown lingered but she went quickly to turn the key and open the door. "What's wrong with knocking—" she began and then broke off as she found him clutching a heavy wooden box. "Can I help?"

He shook his head and edged carefully past her. "I'm sorry to bother you," he added stiffly, "but I forgot to bring the key to my room and I didn't want to leave this in the hall while I went downstairs for a pass key."

"I don't mind—I was just startled." Rosemary was staring with unabashed curiosity at the box, which he'd rested temporarily on the bureau. There was a piece of newspaper over it to keep the contents dry, and since rain was still dripping from his yellow plastic work jacket and slicked-down hair, Daniel had evidently taken his time getting the box from his car.

"Shall I open the bathroom door for you?" she asked finally, trying to sound brisk and efficient.

"What for?"

His abrupt query caught her in mid-step. "Well— I just thought you wanted to take that—whatever it is—" she waved nervously toward the wooden container, "to your room."

He kept a steadying hand on the box but used the other one to rub the back of his neck. "Actually," he said slowly, as if searching for exactly the right words, "I'd thought I might leave it here. If you don't mind."

Remembering his anger earlier, she knew how hard it was for him to request anything of the sort. She walked over to the edge of the bed and sank down upon it because the stiffening in her knees had suddenly given out. "That depends on what's in it." And then, feeling she'd been blasé long enough, her voice went up. "Dammit all—I have a right to know that! Even if I am childish and immature."

He winced. "I thought that would come back to haunt me."

"Well, it was a terrible thing to say. Besides, it isn't true. I didn't know that Simon was going to pick that moment to kiss me. He hadn't made any passes all afternoon."

"Am I supposed to cheer?"

She flushed under his look and dropped her gaze to the shiny pink bedspread beside her. "Forget it. Put the box wherever you want."

There was a moment's silence while Daniel's jaw tightened. Then he said, "Unlock that armoire door, will you? There's a good lock on it so this should be safe enough until morning."

Rosemary walked quickly over to the big oak armoire on the far wall, shoving aside the few clothes she had in it so that he could put the box at the bottom.

As she started to move away, he caught her arm. "I think you're entitled to a look," he said, pulling aside the paper. "You can understand why I didn't want to leave this in the car."

Rosemary's eyes went saucerlike at the contents. "Good Lord! Is that dynamite?"

Daniel nodded grimly.

"Those other things—the funny little capsules with the wires attached—what are they?"

"Blasting caps. And *funny*'s the wrong adjective—believe me."

Rosemary closed her eyes. "This place is getting to me. For a minute I thought I'd seen one before." She threw out her palms in a helpless gesture. "What's next? Hand grenades in the medicine cabinet?"

"Don't be ridiculous." He was tucking the paper carefully back over the top of the box before locking the armoire door and hefting the key. "Do you have a safe place to keep this?"

Startled, Rosemary nodded and instinctively put her hand to her breast.

Daniel's grin was too knowledgeable by far. "That should be safe enough. At least for tonight," he said and gave her the key.

Rosemary's color heightened and every feminine instinct she possessed wanted to quarrel with his assured pronouncement. It was only the niggling suspicion that she'd come out the loser which prompted her silence.

Evidently it was a surprise to Daniel, who hesitated by the bathroom door. He shot her an uncertain look before saying, "If it's all right with you—I'll take the first shift in the shower. There should still be time for us to have a drink before dinner if we get cracking."

Rosemary's annoyance turned to triumph. "You'll have to be a little more explicit. Does this mean you're actually asking me to have dinner with you?"

"I didn't think you needed an engraved invitation." He frowned as another possibility occurred to him. "You haven't got anything planned with Hardy, have you?"

Rosemary thought fast. There was no way she could fake a date under the circumstances. No matter how much she'd like to tell Daniel to go to blazes— this wasn't the time to do it.

Her hesitation had given her away. His expression smoothed as he said, "I'm glad that you finally showed some sense. If this storm gets any worse, it wouldn't be safe driving around. Frankly, I'll be glad to have a chance to relax—it's been a long day."

Rosemary watched him disappear into the bathroom without replying, thankful that they'd achieved a tenuous peace. She felt an instant's remorse that she'd even hesitated accepting his dinner invitation. His clothes showed that he'd spent another weary day underground at Wheal Tamar. If she hadn't been so busy scrapping with him, she would have noticed the tired lines at the corners of his eyes and mouth early on. When they'd first met, he'd shown a casual assurance and determination, but it wasn't until Simon appeared on the scene that his demeanor had changed. And the way he'd behaved on the porch a little earlier showed that his temper had a far shorter fuse than those dynamite caps he'd carried.

Rosemary looked down at the armoire key in her palm and then carefully zipped it into the side of her handbag. Contrary to Daniel's expectations, she had no intention of using another cache just then.

She couldn't resist teasing him about the key he'd left with her when they were in the small bar later waiting for the dining room to open. Running a finger down the stem of her sherry glass, she adopted a terrible Mata Hari accent, saying, "Een case you are vonderink, the key ess safe und zound."

Daniel couldn't have been more startled if she'd suddenly balanced the sherry glass on top of her head. "What the hell!" he started to say, before her meaning penetrated. Then he leaned back, grinning. "I owe you one for that. Before you sidetrack me completely, is it safe to ask where you put it?"

"The key?" She patted her purse suggestively, thinking how nice it was to see him smile. "It's in here."

He grinned wickedly. "Too bad."

His quick recovery almost caught her off guard. "For a minute, I had you going."

"Let's say you startled me." He picked up his Scotch with its one ice cube and swirled the liquid, staring down into the glass. "It's not the first time. Do you have the same effect on everybody?"

"My boss puts it another way—much more graphic and not nearly as complimentary," Rosemary responded. She could have told him that his own presence had done far more than startle her every time they'd met. Whether he was in worn jeans and a work shirt or the well-tailored gray herringbone sport jacket and knitted silk tie he was wearing just then—she could scarcely manage a sensible conversation.

He acknowledged her reply with a quirk of his mouth, but all the while he was staring so intently at her sheer blouse that she wondered if he could see how hard her heart was thumping. It was a relief when he said, "That color is an amazing match for your eyes. It reminds me of the sky when I was driving back here tonight—there was one patch of deep blue just before the storm started." He took a swallow of his drink. "There's a certain similarity there, too."

"And we were doing so well." She shook her head as she pretended to consult her watch. "The armistice has been in effect almost an hour."

He looked amazed. "That was a compliment!"

"It was?" She took a swallow of her sherry. "Maybe I shouldn't have this on an empty stomach—it's corroding my mind."

"Didn't you eat any lunch?"

"Yes, of course—but it was a long time ago. And on the light side. Have you noticed that British sandwiches are undernourished?"

"Of course—but you just order twice as many."

"A woman can't do that—unless she's pretending to be in training as the circus fat lady. The only way to beat the system is to have a whopping afternoon tea." She looked at him sorrowfully and then hiccoughed. "I forgot to have tea."

He pushed her glass back abruptly, saying, "We'll have dinner in a minute—they're opening the dining room now. A bowl of soup will fix you up faster than . . ." he broke off as her shoulders started to shake in convulsive laughter. "You little devil! You're leading me on again! Keep that up and there'll be another part of your anatomy to match that deep blue I was talking about."

"No sense of humor—that's your trouble," she said, unabashed.

He drained his glass and got up, holding out his hand. "Let's go eat. I need strength if I'm going to deal properly with you."

Mrs. Carras seemed inordinately pleased that they were together for dinner and recommended the roast chicken after seating them with a flourish. Rosemary was surprised to find how snug the dining room seemed and mentioned it to Daniel once they'd given their order.

"That's because of the wind direction," he said, nodding toward the partially curtained window beside them. "It must cost them plenty to heat this place during the winter. Somebody could make a fortune selling insulation around Cornwall."

"That's an idea for your next job—if you ever get tired of the mining consultant business."

Daniel buttered a piece of roll, seemingly intent on his task. "After today, I'd apply for the French

Foreign Legion if I had the energy. The ownership of Wheal Tamar is controlled by one family and I think I've spoken to every last cousin and nephew in the last day or so."

"Does the blonde belong to the hierarchy, too?" When he looked up, puzzled, she went on. "The one who drives you to work. Mrs. Carras has mentioned her twice."

"Oh, you mean Win."

"Win? Is that short for Winifred?"

"Nope," he said, shaking his head. "Winsome. She tells me it's an old English name that means attractive." He took a bite of roll. "In her case, it fits."

"I see." So much for a subtle approach, Rosemary thought desolately. She sat immobile while their waitress served the soup, wondering what had suddenly happened to her appetite.

"Win's invited me to her wedding. I'll have to remember to send a gift," he added offhandedly.

Rosemary's head came up. "Who's she marrying?"

"The son of one of the mine's directors. Nice fellow. He's been a big help to me in this investigation—though that isn't surprising. He needs Wheal Tamar to earn a living and now that the management has decided to continue the mine's operation, morale is higher all around."

Rosemary picked up her spoon, her appetite miraculously regained. Beef barley wasn't her favorite soup but she was so intent on Daniel's revelations that she hardly was aware of what she was eating.

"Does that mean that they're going along with all your findings?"

He nodded, and broke off another piece of roll, his lean fingers brushing the crumbs away absently. "The core samples were better than I anticipated and that, together with a vertical retreat . . . there's no point in going into technicalities—but it's a different mining method that should pay off," he finished briskly.

"That's wonderful. I had no idea that all your troubles were over." When he frowned and went on crumbling his roll, she said, "Or is that being too optimistic?"

"Tomorrow should tell." He shot an impatient glance toward the kitchen, as if anxious to end the discussion. "Where in the hell did they go for that chicken?"

"I think the girl's coming with it now," Rosemary said mildly. "You really should take a course in conversational English."

His lips twitched. "What to say until the doctor comes?"

"Or the roast chicken."

"I thought women made that their province." He leaned back in his chair to stare at her, clearly unaffected by her remarks. "Or maybe I'm thinking of seduction."

"You'll have to forgive me if I don't throw myself across the dinner table."

"It *is* a little crowded for that sort of thing. Don't

you think so?" Daniel addressed his question to their young waitress who was serving the chicken.

"Beg pardon, sir?"

"He was just saying that the dining room is crowded tonight," Rosemary cut in desperately.

The girl nodded, her mind on other things. "It always is when the weather's like this. Bother—I forgot the bread sauce."

Rosemary stared accusingly at Daniel after the girl went back to the kitchen. "I liked it better when you didn't have anything to say."

He had trouble keeping a straight face. "Sauce?"

She frowned her disapproval and then saw he was offering a small tureen of cranberry. "Oh! No thank you."

Daniel nodded, apparently intent on his dinner, and Rosemary found the only sensible thing was to follow suit. The waitress returned to leave a dish filled with what appeared to be grainy library paste, and dashed off again.

Without saying anything, Daniel courteously offered it to Rosemary.

She moved the serving spoon In the sticky mixture suspiciously. "All right, I give up. What is it?"

"Sauce. Bread sauce." Daniel dropped his attention back to his creamed potatoes.

"I gathered that." She tried to remain pleasant despite an ever-increasing urge to pour the white mess over his stubborn head. "What do I do with bread sauce? And *don't* say 'eat it.' "

He looked at her solemnly. "I was trying not to say anything at all. You're damned hard to please."

She put down her fork and sat back. "You win again. All right—you have a remarkable gift for conversation. If you can spare a few gems now, tell me what the dickens I do with this wallpaper paste."

"Believe it or not, you *do* eat it. It's a side dish for the chicken."

Rosemary deposited a bit on her plate and tasted it carefully.

"Anybody would think it was pilchard pie complete with fish heads giving you the eye through the top crust," he said watching her.

She shuddered and took another bite.

"Like it?" he wanted to know.

"What's to like? You're sure it's not wallpaper paste?"

"According to experts, it's bread dissolved in hot milk . . ."

"But there's a strange flavor."

"That's because there's an onion skewered by a bunch of cloves in the milk. When you're finished cooking the sauce, you throw away the onion and the cloves. I may have lost something in the translation," he added, trying to be fair.

"You know what I think?"

"Of course—and I agree with you. Wholeheartedly."

"I wondered why you avoided it."

There was a comfortable silence after that while they finished their chicken and vegetables. It wasn't until they were eating a toothsome jam tart for dessert that Rosemary dared go back to the subject that really interested her.

"You said you'd soon know what's been happening at Wheal Tamar. Does that mean that Claire's husband is in the clear?"

"We still have some questions to ask him—mainly, I want to hear his explanation for stashing away that cache of explosives I've got upstairs." Daniel put his fork on the edge of his plate after taking the last bite. "How did you fare with Mrs. Rome today? I presume you did keep your appointment with her."

He didn't bother to hide his sarcasm, showing that he hadn't forgotten Simon's presence earlier. Rosemary pretended to ignore the dangers. "Yes—before lunch. Claire's having production problems. Apparently there's a scarcity of women whom she can hire."

"Does that mean she can't complete her business with you?"

"It's still up in the air. She was going to try and recruit some women today. I'll call tomorrow and learn what happened." Rosemary pushed her plate away and reached for her napkin. "I'm keeping my fingers crossed. Heaven knows what my boss will say if the whole project falls through."

"I thought he was a pretty good sort."

"Oh, he is—" She broke off to ask abruptly, "How did you know?"

Daniel shrugged and got to his feet. "Damned if I

remember. Probably Lance mentioned him. Let's go have coffee in the lounge before it's all gone."

They reached the chilly room where an electric heater was trying to fight the drafts and helped themselves from a carafe of coffee, kept warm by a small container of canned heat. Daniel took a sip from his cup and looked thoughtful.

"What's the matter?" Rosemary wanted to know.

"I was just wondering whether to drink this or pour it over my feet. Let's sit in the corner—it should be warmer away from the windows."

She nodded and sat down beside him on the vinyl couch. "Will you be heading for warmer climates when you leave here?"

He hesitated and then said carefully. "It depends. I'll have to talk to Lance and some other people."

"I see." Her expression was more revealing than she realized. "It's strange but I don't even know where you live—when you're not off on a job somewhere."

"Sometimes I have to check my driver's license to make sure myself."

"But you must go home someplace—"

"There's an apartment in Anchorage and another in Sun Valley where my family lives."

"Family?" she faltered, feeling a cold shaft in her middle that had nothing to do with the Cornwall weather.

"My mother and father." His slow smile was pure amusement this time. "Despite the prevailing opinion, I didn't come out from under a rock. I even have a married sister."

"I didn't know—Lance didn't say anything."

"I'm surprised he didn't get around to it," Daniel replied ruefully. "My partner seems to have been more talkative than usual lately. Maybe getting married has changed his way of thinking."

"There's nothing wrong with matrimony!"

Daniel's eyebrows went up at her vehemence. "I didn't say the change was bad. He's never been happier and I'm beginning to think . . ."

He broke off almost thankfully as Mrs. Carras came toward them, saying, "Miss Lewis—I'm glad to find you here. There's an overseas call for you. You can take it in the office if you like. I've left the door open."

Daniel put his cup down and got up as Rosemary did. "I'll go on upstairs," he said.

Rosemary nodded her thanks to the hotel manageress and went out to the hall with him. "I can't imagine who's calling me. I hope there's nothing wrong."

"Why do women always imagine the worst? Maybe your boss is wondering if you're still earning your salary or a boyfriend is worrying about you." The last was tacked on casually.

"There's nobody who'd call—" Too late she realized that she was giving away more than she'd planned. She managed to smile as they reached the foot of the stairs where they split forces. "Probably it's my aunt, ready to disinherit me for not writing."

"Right. Well, I'll see you later."

Rosemary's eyebrows drew together as he went up the stairs two at a time. Blast the man! For one minute, he was practically admitting that he had marriage on the mind and, in the next, he was casually talking about her mythical boyfriend—one who cared enough for a transatlantic call. Which meant that jealousy hadn't caused his flare-up over Simon earlier. He just didn't like anybody connected with the Rome family—even a relative by marriage.

She was still frowning about that as she reached the empty hotel office and picked up the telephone. "This is Rosemary Lewis."

"One moment, please," came the operator's voice. "Your call is through, sir. Miss Lewis is on the wire."

"Rosie—what the devil's going on over there?"

It didn't take a crystal ball to recognize the voice of her employer behind his opening blast and, a few minutes later, his closing ultimatum was equally clear, despite the thousands of miles between them.

"You're working with a loser, honey. Cut your losses and go on back to London. If this Rome woman ever gets the production bottleneck sorted out—she can contact us. Right now, she'd never make our deadline for the holiday trade. At least, not in the numbers we need."

"Does that mean you want me to fly right home?"

"I'm not sure about that," he said after a perceptible pause. "There are some other prospects on tap. You'd better wait in London for the rest of the week until I can learn whether there's anything worthwhile."

"Why don't I stay close to Claire while I'm waiting? That way I could resolve this contract, as well."

"That's just what you're *not* supposed to do—"

"What do you mean, *supposed* to do?" she cut in. "Who says?"

"I do. Isn't that enough?"

He'd never been that dogmatic before in all the time she'd worked for him. Rosemary tried to keep the hurt from her voice as she said, "I'm sorry. I was just trying to help."

"Dammit, girl—I know that. And I'm an old fogy who's not very good at following a script." His sigh was audible even over the noisy line. "This isn't the time to argue. I want you back in London by tomorrow night. Will you be staying at the same hotel?"

"They said they'd have a room when I came back from Cornwall." She chewed on her lip and finally gave voice to her suspicion. "Did Daniel Harcourt get in touch with you?"

"Who's he? Some friend of yours?"

"Well, he's staying at this hotel," she replied, adopting the same evasive tactics. "He's an American mining consultant. As a matter of fact, he's Lance Fletcher's partner. You must remember meeting Lance and his wife when they dropped in at the office to see me."

"Sure I do." His tone became more affable. "It's a small world. Maybe this Harcourt can help you out—drive you to the station tomorrow. Tourists have to stick together."

"He's not a tourist exactly—he's working here, and I'm certainly not going to ask any favors from him."

"That's up to you—just be in London tomorrow night. In the meantime, I'll tell Lance that I talked to you."

Rosemary heard his receiver go down. She held on to hers for an instant before she put it back on the phone. It was the last remark that kept her there, frowning with indecision, until the solution suddenly made itself clear. How could he tell Lance that he'd called? Unless Lance—a virtual stranger—had instigated the order for her to return to London in the first place. It didn't take a mental giant to fathom that Lance wouldn't have been involved in the proceedings unless he'd been prodded by one Daniel Harcourt!

Rosemary's first impulse was to rush upstairs and confront him with her suspicions. In fact, she was halfway up before she realized that such tactics would accomplish absolutely nothing.

She went on to the top and moved almost reluctantly to her bedroom door, wondering why Daniel had bothered to go to such extremes. If the situation at Wheal Tamar really were so critical that he wanted her out of range, he wouldn't have been discussing the rosy prospects of the mine's future over the dinner table. Logic indicated that he simply didn't want to be bothered with one more minor irritation at such a vital time. Slowly she went into the room, locking the door behind her.

She wasn't astonished to find it empty. She wandered around for a minute after putting her jacket down and then, on an impulse, retrieved the armoire key from her purse and unlocked the cabinet door. Not surprisingly, Daniel's box was exactly where he'd left it.

As she stood there, she could hear the muted sound of the radio from his room. It was a temptation to knock on the door to tell him where he could take his evidence and exactly what he could do with it. Instead, she muttered a heartfelt "Damn" and decided to go to bed—defeated but with her pride still intact.

She was sitting up in bed reading a little later when a knock sounded on her hall door. Her pulse rate leaped but her voice was creditably calm. "What is it?"

Daniel kept his tone low. "I want to talk to you."

All of the anger that she'd managed to submerge surged suddenly to the surface. She swung her legs onto the floor and, pulling on her pale green robe, marched to the door. "It'll have to wait till morning," she announced through the wood. "I'm in bed."

"The hell you are! Let me in before we wake up the whole hotel."

"Why can't you ever take no for an answer?" she asked through clenched teeth. When his fist again thudded on the door, she gritted out, "Stop that. You'll get us thrown out!"

"Not if you unlock this bloody thing!"

"Oh, all right—anything to keep you quiet!" Angrily, she turned the key and yanked the door open.

He moved her aside with a brief, decisive gesture as he came in and closed the door behind him. "What's the big deal about opening a door?" he asked then. "My God, anybody would think I was the Yorkshire killer. All I want is to reclaim my property."

"Oh, I'm sure of that," she countered, matching his sarcasm. "You've made your attitude crystal clear all along. I've never seen a man more dedicated to his job—twenty-four hours a day." She gestured toward the box in the armoire. "Just take it along—and try not to stub your toe when you hide it under your bed. I'd hate to suffer any more because of your schemes."

He froze by the armoire door and turned to face her. In his dark blue robe and matching pajamas, he looked formidable and dangerous. "What's that supposed to mean?"

Her hands went nervously to tighten the belt on her robe, as if the action would strengthen the barricade between them. "You know very well! Are you going to deny that you're behind that long-distance call tonight?"

"It was supposed to come through this afternoon. Unfortunately, it couldn't be completed then because you were out with—Simon."

"You make it sound like a crime. At least I don't go around interfering in your work."

"Good Lord! I didn't get you fired . . ."

"Well, you didn't do badly for a first attempt. I have to give up on Claire's firm and go back to London."

"What's so bad about that?" he asked, watching as she pushed back a strand of hair with an angry gesture. The illumination from a nearby lamp highlighted its coppery color, making it as vibrantly lovely as her slim figure, which she was trying so hard to conceal. He shoved his hands into the pockets of his robe with a decided effort, "You make it sound like heading for the guillotine. Staying in London isn't hard to take."

"That isn't the point and you know it," she flared back. "I've never seen such a man for overlooking the obvious. You've been annoyed ever since I set foot in this hotel but I didn't think you'd be childish enough to really get rid of me."

"Don't be an idiot—you have it all wrong."

"Have I?" Her lips twisted wryly. "You couldn't have been more off-putting if you'd carried a baseball bat. What I don't understand is your high handed attitude."

"Meaning Simon Hardy, I suppose."

"That's right."

"There might be method in my madness if you'd stop and think it over. Oh, the hell with it! I'm not going to argue any longer." Daniel strode over to open the bath's connecting doors so that he could reach his room. "We can settle this all another time," he said as he returned and retrieved the box of dynamite.

Rosemary watched him carry it through the bathroom and carefully deposit it on the floor at the foot of his bed. She was still seething with anger but not so illogical as to disturb his concentration, despite the angry taunt she'd thrown at him earlier.

Daniel's relief was evident when he straightened and turned to face her. "That does it for now. If I don't see you before you leave for London—" he began, only to have her cut in summarily.

"I'm not at all sure that I'm going."

He was back beside her in an instant, yanking the lace-trimmed collar of her robe onto her upper arms to hold her immobile as he glared down at her. "You'll go, damn it! For once in your life, do as you're told!"

"Try and make me!" She struggled in his unrelenting grip, feeling like a gnat attacking armor plate. "Let go of me ... you ... you ... beast!"

"When you learn to follow orders, I'll be glad to. Your boss didn't have any effect, so let's see how this works." He transferred his clasp on her robe to one hand, using the other to catch her chin firmly in his fingers. His mouth descended slowly, and when she would have bit him, he merely tightened his hold. She gasped at his strength, relaxing her lips for one unwary instant. That was all he needed to clamp his mouth possessively over hers in a hard, urgent kiss that went on and on.

Sometime during that mindless interval, his clasp changed to an embrace and he murmured with satisfaction when he pushed aside the lace trimming that had gotten in his way so he could touch her silken skin. As his hands moved expertly over her, seeking and finding, Rosemary pressed even closer, following an instinct stronger than reason or conscious thought. All she knew was that she'd never felt the same with any other man and marveled at the pure joy which enfolded her.

When she finally moved back so that she could breathe, she found that her own hands remained traitorously around Daniel's neck, smoothing and gentling his dark hair with movements as possessive as his own.

She was still so breathless that she couldn't meet his gaze and rested her head against his chest to recover. As she heard Daniel's heartbeat thundering in her ear, her lips curved in wonderment. Apparently his veneer of calm wasn't any deeper than her own and, at that moment, she would have sunk ingloriously onto the Carras Hotel carpet if she hadn't clung to him.

Daniel took a deep breath and finally said, "Evidently I should have tried this approach before."

His voice was uneven but there was definitely an undertone of laughter.

"Ummm," was all Rosemary could manage in return. It took almost ten seconds before his remark penetrated and then she shoved back so fast that Daniel had to steady himself against the wall or lose his balance.

"What the dickens—" he began.

"You mean that's all it was to you?" she interrupted, her breast heaving. "Just another angle! And I was supposed to be so impressed that I'd do anything you wanted?"

Daniel rubbed his face wearily as he stared down at her. "I told you that I didn't have time to explain."

"Just say yes or no. Was this another trick?"

"You don't really expect me to answer that."

She stared at him desolately, aware that he had no intention of doing anything but stand like a stone pillar, with about as much expression on his face, for the rest of the night, if necessary. She retreated another step, struggling to keep her voice level. "All this—just so I'd take the London train tomorrow. Am I right?"

"I hoped I could persuade you to use your head," he acknowledged, his tone deep and bitter. "You didn't seem to object when Simon used the same tactics in the car tonight. Did you question his motives? Or did he have a better technique?"

"Go to hell," Rosemary said tonelessly and clenched her fists at her side as she turned away.

She didn't move again until she'd heard both bathroom doors close behind him, and she didn't make a sound as she walked across her room. She didn't start to cry until she'd sagged onto the bed and could use one of the hard Carras Hotel pillows to muffle her despair.

Chapter Seven

The night seemed endless. Rosemary remained curled in an unhappy heap even when her hot water bottle turned cool and the sheets became glacial. Not for anything would she have gotten up and stumbled to the bathroom trying for hot water, possibly awakening Daniel while doing so. She'd carry off the pretense of not giving a damn if she froze in the process!

Despite her forebodings of such a dire end, she fell asleep toward morning when she resorted to counting the gusts of wind rattling her window rather than Cornish sheep. She was awakened a little later by the early tea service along the corridor, frowning when she heard the cart go past both her room and Daniel's without stopping. She didn't miss starting the day with lukewarm tea; it was the silence from the room next door that had her wondering.

The quiet prevailed for the next half-hour—a time when normally Daniel would be showering and dressing for work. Rosemary lay immobile, groggy

164

from her lack of sleep but alert enough to wonder what was happening.

Finally she couldn't stand the suspense any longer and got out of bed. She wrapped a blanket around her shoulders to combat the chilled room, wincing as she saw the lace-trimmed robe which Daniel had manhandled earlier. She'd never be able to wear it again without thinking of that painful episode. Shaking her head ruefully, she tiptoed to the bathroom and then, making sure it was empty, continued to Daniel's connecting door. She opened it the barest crack and peeked around it. The single bedspread was wrinkled but the linen was undisturbed. Sometime in the early-morning darkness, Daniel had evidently packed his belongings, shouldered his box of explosives, and checked out.

Mrs. Carras confirmed it when Rosemary descended for breakfast a little later.

"My word, you Americans start moving early," she said, leading the younger woman to her usual table by the window. "Mr. Harcourt was gone even before I was up this morning—he left a note on my desk saying that he'd changed his plans."

"Did he leave a forwarding address?" When the hotel woman looked puzzled, Rosemary fumbled for an excuse. "I just wondered if you knew where to send his bill."

"Mr. Harcourt settled that early on. The account is always sent to his London business address. He said he'd be responsible for yours, as well."

"No way! I mean—I'll take care of it myself. Thanks just the same."

Mrs. Carras continued to linger even after she'd put the typed breakfast menu on the table. "Mr. Harcourt's note mentioned that you'd be checking out today, too. Is that right?"

By then, Rosemary was too tired to carry her crusade for independence any further. Eventually she'd leave to go back to London, and after that, take a welcome plane home. Maybe after she'd put six thousand miles between her and that six-foot example of high handed masculine arrogance, she'd be able to call her soul her own again.

"I could use the room," Mrs. Carras went on haltingly. "Somehow, I made a mistake on our reservation list. Mind you, I could shift some guests around, if you want to stay. In case Mr. Harcourt was wrong."

"He's never wrong. I learned that first thing." Rosemary picked up the menu and then put it down again as the smell of kippers floated in from the kitchen. She closed her eyes for an instant as her stomach protested the strong, fishy odor and opened them again to find Mrs. Carras giving her a concerned look.

"Is there anything wrong, Miss Lewis?"

Rosemary managed a reassuring smile. "Not a thing. I was just thinking that I've been eating too much since I came to Cornwall."

"No kippers this morning?"

"No kippers."

"Fried egg and bread with a rasher of bacon?"

Rosemary shook her head again as the smell of burning bacon wafted through to mingle with the kipper. "Tea and toast will do it. And some of that nice marmalade."

"I'll see to it myself." Mrs. Carras lingered long enough to add, "And I'll have your account ready when you want to check out. Shall I call you a taxi?"

Rosemary had visions of sitting on the hotel steps with her bags half-packed and decided that enough was enough. "I'll call one when I'm all set and I've decided which train to catch."

Despite moving at a leisurely pace after breakfast, it didn't take Rosemary long to pack her belongings and be ready to check out. She consulted her pocket-sized British Rail schedule and discovered that she would have no trouble with transportation to London. There was excellent train service from the peninsula. Too good—so she couldn't use that as an excuse for lingering in Truro.

She went down to the office and used the phone to call Claire Rome—hoping a final contract signing could prove a legitimate excuse to stay over. After all, there were other hotels nearby and it would serve Daniel right to learn that he hadn't the final word! She'd go back to London when *she* decided.

Her splendid decision was doomed to disaster when the Rome number rang and rang without answer. Rosemary frowned as she waited, wondering why Claire would leave without calling as she'd promised. Of course, the woman could have simply gone grocery shopping with a neighbor, planning to get in touch later with a report on developments.

Unfortunately, it didn't help as a delaying tactic. She hung up, still resolved that she wasn't going to take a morning train. The thought of sitting in an empty London hotel room for the rest of the day held no attraction. If she could wait until afternoon, it would be evening when she arrived in London and she could hole up with the BBC for company. "Probably there'll be another snooker championship on television," she told herself bitterly, "or a fascinating documentary on the evolution of man."

Mrs. Carras was behind the reception desk when Rosemary went out into the hall a little later. "At least the storm has blown itself out so you'll have a better day for traveling," the hotel woman said cheerily. "All set, are you?"

"Not exactly. I've had to change my plans a little. Oh, nothing to interfere with your reservations," Rosemary added hurriedly when a worried look came over the other's face. "I'd just like to leave my luggage here for a while—if it won't be in the way. I'll pick it up later. And now I'd appreciate it if you'd call a taxi for me."

"Of course, I'll be glad to. But perhaps I'd best wait until you chat with your young man."

"My what?" Rosemary's frown eased as she turned to see Simon vaulting up the front steps of the hotel. "For heaven's sake—now what?"

"I *am* glad I caught you," he said, sounding

breathless as he came in the door. "From the looks of things, I'm just in time. Surely you can take a later train and have a coffee with me?"

"Actually, I wasn't headed for the train. Mrs. Carras was just going to call a taxi for me. I wanted to go back toward Land's End and finish my sightseeing."

"I can take over on that score." He bestowed a beaming smile on both of them and held open the front door for Rosemary. "And I'll even buy you a coffee in the bargain to celebrate the end of our stormy weather. I like this sunshine much better."

They were halfway down the steps before Rosemary managed to call a halt. "Hold on a minute—you're going too fast. Now what's all this about?"

His smile faltered and for an instant he looked like a small boy who saw a cherished prize slipping from his grasp. "Nothing special. But after yesterday, I just thought it would be nice if we could spend some time together. You didn't tell me you were going to leave today."

She flushed at his reproof and hurried to explain. "I wouldn't have gone without saying good-by. Actually, I tried to call Claire a few minutes ago but there wasn't any answer."

He urged her gently on toward his car, which he'd parked at the curb. "She went out earlier. I told her that I'd be seeing you, so she didn't have to feel guilty on that score."

"Did she have any luck yesterday?"

Simon brushed back her hair with a teasing gesture as she turned an eager face. "I'd call it encouraging but you'll have to talk to her later on. Do you know—that's the most interest you've shown since I arrived. What does a chap have to do to impress an American career woman?"

She pretended to think. "I sell out pretty cheap. Maybe for the price of a cup of coffee—if you were serious about your offer."

"Am I!" He hurriedly unlocked the car door and almost pushed her inside. "In case you're thinking of changing your mind."

Rosemary waited until he'd come around and was seated beside her before she gestured toward her blazer and skirt. "Will I be warm enough? I know the sun's shining now but I don't have much faith in your Cornish weather."

He was starting the car, and turned to smile at her. "Don't worry, I'll put the heater on if you get chilly, and there's always my mac. It's still on the back seat. I won't need it."

Rosemary gave an approving glance at his dark gray suit. "You look much too elegant for driving around the suburbs. Are you sure that you don't have other things to do?"

"As a matter of fact—I do. But there's no hurry. What's at the top of your sightseeing list?"

"It isn't at all important . . ."

Simon made a production of pulling to the curb and slowing almost to a stop. "I think I should be the one to decide that."

"Well, if you must know—I was going to hire a

taxi to take me to that open-air theatre we passed yesterday."

His brows drew together. "The Minack at Porthcurno? But that's almost to Land's End itself." A grin slowly spread over his thin face. "I hope you planned to ask the fare first."

"Of course. I know it sounds silly but I didn't want to leave Cornwall without seeing the place and I thought I could take an afternoon train to London."

Simon braked completely, letting the engine idle. Since the street was bare of traffic at that hour and there were no pedestrians on the tree-lined sidewalk, it was as if they had the world to themselves. Another part of the Cornish charm, Rosemary thought, and one that she hated to leave.

"What's the great hurry to get to London?" Simon wanted to know. "It doesn't seem to be your idea."

"Orders from my boss. He phoned last night." She was tempted to explain Daniel's part in the ultimatum but discretion triumphed at the last minute. "There are some things I have to do in London."

"Couldn't your friend Harcourt take you around today?"

Rosemary shot Simon a startled glance, thinking that he was either clairvoyant or close to it. "I didn't ask him," she said blithely. "He's too busy most of the time for any larking around. Or so I gather."

"I also gather that you've had a bit of a dustup." Simon's tone was triumphant and he made no attempt to hide his pleased expression as he pulled away from the curb again. "All the better for me. Larking around is second nature in my scheme of things. Let's have our coffee, shall we? Then—on to Porthcurno."

They had their coffee in a sheltered restaurant patio, located in a village which was part cliffside, part harborside on the southern edge of the peninsula. The town had an unpronounceable Cornish name and the small restaurant followed suit. Most of the customers were elderly fishermen who drank their coffee quickly so they could get back to the nearby concrete pier and sort out their lines with renewed vigor.

"Almost as if they felt guilty sitting here and being lazy," Rosemary said, her eyes alight with laughter as she watched a bearded man hurry back to his station. "Or maybe they just like to fish."

"They do. Especially when the sun's out," Simon said, spooning more lumpy demerara sugar into his coffee from a blue-and-white bowl. "At this time of year, good weather in these parts slips through your fingers faster than silver."

"Do they mine silver in Cornwall, too?" she asked idly. "Or is it all tin these days?"

"You should ask your friend Harcourt. He's the expert," Simon drawled. "But he's a dicey subject right now, isn't he? What happened between you two last night? Did he push his claim too far?"

Rosemary couldn't hide her annoyance. She shoved back her cup and reached for her purse. "It's only on the daytime soaps that Americans go from bed to bed—commonly called bed to worse."

When he frowned, uncomprehending, she shrugged. "Sorry—it's an old joke. We'll have to order another cup of coffee if we stay here much longer. The waiter's giving us the eye."

Simon rose from his chair. "And besides you don't want to discuss anything personal."

"That's right. Do you mind?"

He smiled and put a hand on her shoulder as they walked back to the car. "Of course not. But I rather hoped you might trust me by now."

She kept her gaze on the ground, ostensibly watching her footing on the rough, cobblestoned surface of the car park, which was just across a narrow street from the restaurant. When they pulled up so he could unlock the passenger door, she said, "There's really nothing to explain. I told you before, some mutual friends asked Daniel to look after me in Cornwall—that's all."

By then, Simon had gotten behind the wheel. "If you say so. When he came to Claire's house that morning—he gave a different impression."

She shrugged and waited for him to start the car and pull out onto the road. "Probably he didn't want me to get involved while I was here. Just as a matter of principle—"

"Nothing personal, eh?" Simon shot her a quick cynical look. "That wasn't the way it looked from my side of the path."

"Maybe it was all part of his plan."

"And when he kissed you?"

"Oh, for heaven's sake! You kissed me, too. Let's not make a federal case out of it. Those things just happen—" Her voice faltered for an instant and she half-turned to get a better view of his profile. "Although afterwards I thought it might have been part of *your* plan."

His smile appeared briefly but he kept his attention on the road ahead. "You're not only beautiful but you're a downy bird, as well. It was too good a chance to miss—with your chaperon standing there grinding his teeth."

"Men!"

"We have our moments."

His tone was so smug that Rosemary burst out laughing and said, "It's just as well that I'm leaving. Being a bone in the middle is not my idea of fun." A sudden shadow on the field at the right of the road made her lean forward and peer through the windshield. "There's a helicopter. I wonder what's going on."

"Probably it's from the air-sea rescue installation not far from here—one of the bigger ones in Britain," Simon said as the craft turned back toward the north. "Might have been a training mission."

"Isn't there a commercial helicopter service from Cornwall to the Scilly Isles?"

"That's right. Or you can make the thirty-mile trip by sea. At this time of year, you might do better flying."

"It might be best to skip the whole idea if there

were a storm like last night." She sat back in her seat. "I'll have to see the islands on another trip."

"There are better places to go for my money. That's what I wanted to talk about but we can discuss it when we're at the theatre."

He slowed the car as they came upon an intersection where a weathered wooden sign for the Minack Theatre pointed to a track heading toward granite cliffs.

It was like cutting across a vacant field, Rosemary thought, and hung on to the door handle as the car lurched through potholes and over rocks on the gravel lane. She twisted to check their route. "Didn't we pass this turn-off yesterday on the way to Land's End?"

"That's right. It's not far away." Simon swore under his breath as a front wheel slid into a hole that jolted the undercarriage. "This track goes to hell after the end of the season."

"Are you talking about the theatre season or the weather?"

"Both. There won't be any maintenance until the crowds come again in the summer." He gave a grunt of satisfaction as they pulled up near the edge of the hill, against a chain which served as a rough parking barrier. "One good thing—we won't have to worry about being bothered by tourists."

"That's an understatement. There doesn't seem to be anybody around for miles." As he cut the ignition, Rosemary opened her door but lingered to ask,

"Is it all right to wander around the place when the theatre's officially closed?"

"There's nothing to steal. You'll see what I mean when we get down there. Even that ticket hut over there at the top of the stairs is boarded up for the season." He gestured as he got out on his side. "Don't bother to lock your door—we won't be away long. And you'd better let me hang on to you," he cautioned, taking her elbow as they reached a rough path that had stone steps cut into it a little further on. "The heels of those shoes could get you in trouble."

Rosemary drew in her breath sharply as they reached the edge of the cliff where the path descended steeply on the other side. Below them on the right there was a large stone amphitheatre literally carved out of the rock hillside. The semicircles of stone seats for the audience provided excellent viewing for the narrow stage still further down, because there was such a drop between the rows that even the biggest hat or bubble hairdo wouldn't prove a hazard. A hundred or so feet beyond the stone pillars and low bulwark which edged the stage, the gray-blue waters of the Atlantic surged against the shore.

Rosemary made an uneasy sound as she surveyed the awesome scene. "The first step's a dilly from here. If there were a temperamental ingenue in the cast, it wouldn't be hard for the stage director to get rid of her."

"Or a drunk in the audience," Simon agreed, making a scooping motion with his hand.

Rosemary shivered and then suddenly realized it wasn't entirely the subject matter that caused it. "This wind's stronger than I thought. Can you hang on a minute? I'll just dash back to the car and get your raincoat—if you don't mind?"

"Of course not. I'd be happy to get it for you, though."

She shook her head and started back the way they'd come, saying over her shoulder, "My fault. I should have remembered. Be right back."

Once by herself, her features lost their determinedly cheerful expression and settled into a more somber cast. It was all very well to pretend while she was with Simon, but she knew it was a futile gesture. Cornish sightseeing, which had been so enjoyable at Tintagel, suddenly held all the appeal of a trip to the dentist. The worst part was that she suspected London would be exactly the same when she returned. And all because of one man who was more interested in his miserable box of dynamite than he was in her.

Rosemary yanked open the car door with more violence than necessary and reached for Simon's folded raincoat on the seat. When she removed it, she saw that it was covering a now familiar attaché case. She smiled wryly, remembering how it had spilled on the floor that first night he'd picked her up at the station. And how annoyed he'd been—probably because the contents showed he wasn't nearly as neat and tidy as he liked to pretend.

In the middle of shrugging into his coat and rolling up the sleeves, she stopped suddenly to stare down at the case, remembering what she'd seen that night. If it hadn't been for Daniel's box of dynamite—her memory would never have been triggered at all.

Of course Simon could have a perfectly good explanation—and probably did. All the same, she thought as she slowly cinched the raincoat belt, it wouldn't hurt to ask.

"What's wrong. Aren't you coming?"

Simon's hail made her blink and turn to wave reassuringly at him. She slammed the car door and started back down the track, her head downbent.

If only she'd thought about that damned attaché case earlier, she could have asked Daniel if it had any significance. That would have shown him that she wasn't entirely witless, although she'd done her best to convince him just the opposite with her actions.

"I say—what happened to you?" Simon asked when she approached him a minute later. "Is there something wrong with the coat?"

"No—it's fine." She smiled nervously up at him and decided she'd do better with her probing if she were sitting down. "How about a reserved seat? Maybe one with a view of that beach over there."

"Right you are." He vigorously dusted off a stone seat which partially faced the direction she'd indicated. "You have good taste. That's Porthcurno Beach—the place is chock-full of people in summer."

Rosemary huddled into his raincoat as a gust of

wind swirled dust from the path. "In this weather, it's hard to imagine anyone swimming. Does the water ever get warm?"

He shrugged. "It must. Claire and Edwin have been down there. It's not my way of doing things, I must say."

"I'm beginning to wonder exactly what your way is," she said, keeping her voice casual. "Certainly not small-town. How did you happen to surface in Truro instead of London?"

"Beggars can't be choosers." His tone was terse. "I needed a bolt-hole just then and Claire was handy. But I've had enough of family doings now. Edwin's caught up in a bit of a mess from what I gather. That may be all right for Claire but I'm not stuck with the man—so I'm getting out. While there's still time."

"What do you mean—still time? What did he do?"

"I'm not sure. But you can bet he couldn't pull it off and, knowing my brother-in-law, he'd probably expect me to arrange for his defense. I have no intention of throwing good money after bad. He's not the brightest soul around."

"I see."

"No, you don't." Simon reached for her hand and pulled it onto his thigh, covering it with a warm, possessive grasp. "I'm asking you to come with me, love. We'll find someplace where the climate's healthier."

"But I'm going home next week," Rosemary said,

using the only excuse that came to mind in her surprise.

"Good! We'll go together." His clasp tightened even more. "We'd make a smashing team. Who knows what we could turn our mind to."

"You make it sound more like a business venture than matrimony," she said, trying to extricate her hand. Then, seeing his expression change, "Or was it matrimony that you had in mind?"

"There's no reason why it couldn't be," he said, rallying quickly. "We wouldn't need to plunge into it—"

"Maybe get to know each other first," she finished for him when his voice petered out.

"That's right. I knew you'd understand. What do you say, darling?"

"Forget it." She managed to get her hand back and stood up abruptly. "I don't know what you're planning, Simon, but it's a far cry from love and 'happy ever after.'"

"You haven't given me a chance," he protested. Before she knew what he was doing, he'd pulled her back down beside him on the bench. "I may not have brought a special license with me, but if it's action you want . . ."

His mouth fastened over hers with such force that her head was pushed back against his shoulder and she tasted the salty ooze of blood on her lips. As she strained to push away, his hand moved on her thigh with unmistakable possessiveness.

"Simon, for heaven's sake!" She finally writhed

out of his embrace and retreated toward the stone steps. "Just take me back to the hotel."

He threw out his hands in an angry gesture. "My God! There's no pleasing you. First you complain because everything's too businesslike and then you have a fit because somebody lays a finger on you."

"Many more of your fingers and I'd end up with as many bruises as Claire . . ." Rosemary's indignant response was pure impulse. It took his abruptly hardening features to make her think again. "My lord," she said, almost under her breath, "*you* were the one who must have hit Claire that morning. It wasn't her husband at all. And she didn't even let on . . ."

"Because she knew what would happen if she did." Simon stood up with a careless movement, although there was nothing relaxed about his expression. He seemed to be aware of every breath Rosemary took as she stayed facing him at the end of the narrow row. Behind her the sharp-edged steps led upward to the top of the hill or down to the curving stone stage some fifty feet below. Beyond the stairs, there was only rough turf to another vantage point with a low balustrade, over the rocky cove of Porthcurno Beach far below.

At that moment, a sea bird swooped down the edge of the granite cliff, and its mournful cry floated upward on the wind.

The silence following it hadn't lasted more than a second or two before Simon said softly, "Rosemary, there's no need for all this. What happened between me and Claire is over—we understand each other. You know what families are. When people are closely involved, there are bound to be disagreements."

Rosemary moved back far enough to feel the edge of the stone step on her calf but didn't risk any other action as Simon kept his glance steadily on her. "Does that apply to her husband, too?"

"What do you know about Edwin? What did Harcourt say? Tell me." He moved quickly on the last words and clutched her elbow painfully.

"N-nothing," Rosemary stuttered. "He didn't tell me anything. It was just your briefcase."

The words were no sooner out than she could have wept with frustration, because Simon's grasp on her elbow became even more excruciating.

"What in the hell's *that* supposed to mean?" The pain etched on her pale face must have made him realize that if he wanted an answer, he was going about it in the wrong way. His grasp loosened slightly but he kept his hand warningly on her arm. "I want to know about the briefcase."

"It was that first night when you picked me up at the station. The case spilled in the back seat."

"Go on."

"I saw those things with the wires on them. They didn't mean anything to me then. Not until I saw some others just like them last night and learned they were dynamite caps."

"You were with Harcourt last night." Simon made

it a statement, not a question. "So you told him all about it."

She couldn't decide whether it was better to let him think Daniel suspected his involvement or let it coast for the moment. At least until she was able to get back to Truro or into the car. Anywhere but this damned cliff, she thought desperately, and tried to keep her glance from wandering so that Simon wouldn't know how terrified she was. One little push by him and there'd only be a broken body for the waves to wash up thirty seconds later.

"So that's why there was a tail on Edwin when he left for work this morning," Simon was going on, as if thinking out loud. "I told him his luck was about to run out."

"It's not surprising. They found some of the things that he'd left lying around," she said. "I gather the owners of Wheal Tamar take a dim view of having their tunnels blown to smithereens. Even by an expert."

"Oh, Edwin's talented at his job. I'll have to give him that. Unfortunately, the man has no scope for other things."

She stared, appalled by his casual comment. "You call wholesale destruction a talent? I'd say he was a hard-core crazy."

"That depends on your point of view. Edwin got hungry for some of the mine profits. Considering the life he and Claire lead, it's not surprising." Simon spoke offhandedly, apparently disassociating himself from his relatives. Only his voice showed that he wasn't as worldly as he appeared. "I was damned if I'd be caught in that trap again."

"Again?" she asked, trying to sound interested.

It seemed best to keep him talking. Besides, she didn't know what else to do. Not until there was some interruption to distract him so she could try and get back to the car. There was the hope, however faint, that some other fool tourist might pull into the parking lot above. Simon wasn't reckless enough to try anything in front of witnesses.

"I told you about the company I worked for in the Midlands," he was going on in an aggrieved tone. "When they went bankrupt, it was easy for them to put the blame on me. But they weren't able to make the charges stick and nobody will this time, either. Edwin can talk his head off but there's no proof."

"What about Claire?"

His expression sharpened. "What about her? She'll keep her mouth shut if she wants to stay healthy. It only took a little persuasion before . . ."

"So I noticed."

Rosemary wondered how she could ever have thought that his smile was attractive. There wasn't one iota of humor that reached his eyes.

"And much good it will do you, my dear," he informed her smugly. "It's all hearsay—not one bit of solid evidence."

"What about that exploration report that reached Wheal Tamar? The one that cited a dismal economic future. You must have had to pay off some-body for that."

He laughed aloud. "I must say—you try hard. Do you honestly think that any consultant firm will admit filing a dishonest report? Why in the hell should they? They merely stated that, in their opinion, the economic future at Wheal Tamar was unsound."

Suddenly Rosemary felt as if the entire web of deceit was tightening around her. "You can talk all you want about circumstantial evidence, but I'm not going to change *my* mind. I did see those dynamite caps in your attaché case."

"All I have to say is that my brother-in-law put them there to implicate me. He's done so many idiotic things that one more wouldn't be out of character. In fact, I shouldn't be surprised if the authorities haven't got him nicely stuffed away in a mental ward by now," Simon said with a quick glance at his watch. "Especially if he tells them about the van."

"My God, you mean there's more to this horror?"

"Relax, love—you're in no danger from that. I should imagine that he parked it near the headframe at the mine—where it can do the most damage."

"You're still talking in riddles . . ."

"Not at all. Edwin wanted a bargaining point in case the authorities finally caught up with him. He filled a van with petrol and dynamite and wired it so that he can ignite it by remote control. I shouldn't wonder but what he's managed to arrange the same thing in another of the mine tunnels. The man's a

genius when he sets his mind to it." Simon took in
her aghast expression with an almost pitying look.
"So you see, my dear Rosemary, you're well and
truly caught. If you use your head though, the pun-
ishment needn't be harsh. You can give me a nice
holiday in the States and time to get reestablished.
There's no reason we couldn't part friends eventually. But you'll have to make up your mind quickly.
I plan to be in London this evening and at
Heathrow shortly after that."

"And if I don't agree to your plans?" she asked,
trying to keep her voice steady.

He pursed his lips thoughtfully before they curved
in another mirthless smile. "It's a big step down to
the beach," he said, showing he hadn't forgotten
where they were. "I can't take the chance of being
thwarted by a silly twit who doesn't know when to
keep her mouth closed. It would be really easier to
just make sure it's shut—permanently." His hand
tightened painfully on her arm again. "Shall we have
a go at it?"

Rosemary tried not to panic in his bruising grasp.
The only way to keep her sanity just then was to
concentrate on the fine dust nearby, which was trans-
formed into miniature dervishes every time a gust of
wind swept the hillside. "You'll have to let me
think..."

"I'm waiting," Simon said in an uncaring tone
which was more chilling than anything she'd ever
heard.

"All right. Let's go back to the car."

He uttered a breathy sound of triumph and would have kissed her if she hadn't slumped against him, pretending a faintness which wasn't far from real. He wasn't happy about that, and towed her up the stone steps at a pace which had her gasping. Even as they reached the boarded-up ticket hut near the top of the hill, he didn't slacken his stride. Rosemary didn't attempt to linger by the programs and post-cards on display at the hut, keeping her attention on the parking area, which came into view as they finally reached the top of the path.

She wouldn't have believed that anything could have made her even more unhappy at that point, but the sight of that rough patch of land, still unoccupied by anything other than Simon's parked car, sent her hopes plummeting.

He heard her muffled moan of despair and angrily twisted her wrist to hurry her along. "You'd better stop hoping for miracles and settle for what you've got! And take that dismal look off your face—I like my birds to have a bit of style! Just get in the car and—what the bloody hell!"

He shouted the last as a shrill whistle rent the air behind them. As he whirled to see what caused it, Rosemary yanked free and plunged toward the car. After reaching it, she remembered that Simon still had the ignition key and she swerved around the fender as she heard his angry yell.

Before she could look over her shoulder to see how close he was, she saw a masculine figure come around the car and reach out for her. To her glazed, frantic glance he was one other threat to freedom. She screamed and stumbled as she attempted to avoid him, falling heavily onto the rough grass.

From then on, the only realities were the dusty, dank smell of the grass under her face and the grit which cut into her palms as she struggled up again. She tried to blot out the terrifying figure of the man bending over her until his words finally penetrated. "Hang on, darling! Everything's all right. You're safe now."

"Not with Simon here," she said fretfully, trying to explain. "He's to blame—don't let him get away." Then, as her eyes finally focussed on the familiar face so close to hers, she murmured, "Daniel! Oh, thank God!"

"You said it!" His sigh of relief was heartfelt. "Damned if I'm not almost a basket case, too."

She sagged against him, finally noticing Simon in the custody of two uniformed policemen down by the ticket booth. "I—I don't understand. Where did they come from?" She turned her bewildered face up to Daniel who, by then, was gently brushing the grit from her palms with his handkerchief. "Where did *you* come from?"

"I'll explain it all later. Right now, let's just get out of here—as far away as possible from that excuse for a human being." Daniel's voice was rough with emotion. "I warned you about him, and when you get your strength back—"

"I know—you'll make me pay." She managed a tremulous smile. "I'm ready to leave, too. If I never see another Cornish landmark, it'll be too soon." She had to swallow before she could add, "I—I was scared to death. Simon talked about throwing me over the cliff . . . and Edwin was wiring vans with dynamite to blow people up . . ."

"Don't think about it." Daniel frowned at her exhausted tone and tightened his protective clasp on her shoulders. "It's over now. And if you can make it, we'll walk back to the road. There should be another police car any time now. They said a backup unit was on the way."

"But why can't we take this car? Surely the police won't mind if you turn it in when we get back to Truro." She snatched a glimpse of Simon as he was being handcuffed. "I want to get rid of his raincoat—I'll leave it on the back seat."

Daniel held her back as she got up and started toward the small sedan. "For God's sake, stay here, will you! You can pitch that coat to the seagulls if you want—but stay away from the car."

She stared at him, perplexed. "I don't understand—why are you making such a fuss about his car, for heaven's sake?"

"Because when Edwin was telling all at the police station, he not only bragged about wiring the van and the main tunnel—so he could detonate them by remote control—he added a crowning touch. Apparently he was sick and tired of taking Simon's orders, so he decided to show him who was the real boss of the operation." As Rosemary stared at him with a horrified air of discovery, Daniel nodded grimly. "You're right, he'd also wired Simon's car with explosives, just in case. The only thing he wouldn't tell us was his timing schedule—exactly when he'd fixed it to blow."

Chapter Eight

Rosemary collapsed against him and Daniel had to bend his head to hear her repeating tremulously, "I am not going to faint—I am *not* going to faint."

"I'm glad to hear it," he told her brusquely, after deciding that sympathy wasn't going to help just then. "For one thing, there's more gravel than grass on the ground here, and I couldn't carry you all the way to the road without help."

She started to laugh helplessly, aware that tears were still streaming down her cheeks as she burrowed her face in his chest. "Some hero! You're supposed to do better than that."

He caught her arm and started walking toward the road again, content that he'd diverted her, at least temporarily, from the horror she'd endured. "All right, then. You can faint once we've gotten back to the hotel. How about a good half-hour collapse before we leave for London? After that . . ."

"After that I'll probably wake up and find that this has been a bad dream." She shook her head, scarcely believing that they were talking such nonsense as they followed the two policemen who were marching Simon down the rough track. "It would be better that way."

Daniel tightened his hold on her shoulders. "At least there's a happy ending. A little earlier today, I would have been glad to settle for that."

Rosemary managed a crooked smile. "You're not usually a man for half-measures."

He gave her a level look that would have unnerved her even in normal circumstances. "Maybe I've changed."

She pulled up and shaded her eyes as she pretended to scan the sky over Porthcurno Beach. "Good Lord! That remark made Madgy Figgy fall off her broomstick."

He started to laugh, flicking the end of her nose with a teasing finger. "There's only one witch around here. And Madgy rode on ragwort, you idiot—not a broomstick." His voice relaxed even more as he noticed another police car pull in at the end of the track. "Hallelujah! There's our backup unit. The bomb disposal unit is due right behind them. We won't have any trouble getting transportation back to Truro." He cocked a mocking eyebrow at her. "If you've done enough sightseeing for the day."

She had to be satisfied with a withering look; she couldn't risk any more under the benign gaze of four policemen. "You haven't changed at all. Just wait until we get back to the hotel!"

Considering the circumstances, the drive back to

Truro was a blessed calm after the storm. It gave both of them a chance to relax, as their police escorts seemed determined to keep the conversation on a pleasant, uncomplicated level. They didn't refer to Wheal Tamar or Simon at all until they had finally driven up in front of the Carras, ready to let Rosemary and Daniel out.

"We'll be in touch for your statement, Miss Lewis," the younger one said. "There's some other testimony we need to get first so don't worry if it takes a day or two."

"Does that mean I have to stay here?"

"Not at all. We told Mr. Harcourt that earlier. You can sign a deposition in London or wherever."

"You'll need my address and phone."

"Mr. Harcourt took care of that, too," he said, touching the bill of his uniform cap. "We have his business number in London."

"Yes, but what about my . . ."

". . . that's taken care of, too," Daniel said, getting out of the car and pulling her behind him before she could finish her sentence. Bending down to close the door, he said to the officers, "Thanks again for all your help. It's been quite an experience."

"I should say it was the other way around," the older policeman said. "We're most grateful for your assistance." His glance toward Rosemary was kind and reassuring. "The best of British luck, Miss Lewis. You should enjoy the rest of your holiday."

"I can testify to that," Daniel said, towing her into the hotel after the car drove off.

"Wait a minute—I don't have a room here. I've already checked out."

"We're going up to my room," he said, ushering her up the stairs. "Mrs. Carras told me to leave my things there when I was trying to locate you earlier. I'll collect them and check out again. For good, this time."

"I didn't know you were going back to London, too," she said happily as she followed him in the door. "Or am I taking too much for granted?"

He stopped to smile at her—a lovely warm, slow smile that made her tingle all the way to her toes. "Not bloody likely, as the British say. You haven't taken a single thing for granted since we met."

"And whose fault is that?" When he started toward her, she smiled but shook her head. "First things first. I'm going to sit here on this splendid bed and watch you pack—while you explain what happened today. How did you know where to find me?"

"Thank Mrs. Carras for that. She told us what she overheard when Simon arrived, and we started toward Land's End after you. By then, the police had brought in a helicopter to speed up the search. Once the pilot radioed that he'd located Simon's car—it didn't take us long." Daniel paused to fold a sweater and drop it in the top of his bag. "Which was a damned good thing because we couldn't take chances on Edwin Rome's rantings. He isn't exactly the stable type."

"And Claire? Was she in on it, too?"

Daniel shook his head sympathetically. "I think

she did everything possible to stop both her brother and her husband. I don't know whether you're aware of it or not but it was Simon who pushed her around that morning—that was another reason Edwin was so unstrung."

"Then maybe when this is over, Claire can still salvage something of her marriage and her career."

"We'll hope so. At least her career." Daniel zipped his suit bag closed. "I think that's everything."

"Hold on a minute. I still want to know what gave Simon the idea for all this."

"According to his brother-in-law, Simon's been the kind who pulled strings all his life while taking care to avoid the dirty work. Incidentally, he wasn't lily-white in that bankruptcy of his former firm—they just couldn't get a conviction on the embezzling charges against him. Anyhow, when he came down to Cornwall, he decided to try for even bigger stakes and get control of Wheal Tamar. We still don't know who helped bankroll him, but the authorities think they will very soon. Simon had learned how to falsify accounting procedures and it wasn't hard to do after Edwin introduced him to a girl who worked in that department of the mine. She confessed at our first questioning because Simon promised her marriage and made her settle for a lot less."

Rosemary grimaced sympathetically. "Hell hath no fury . . ."

"Exactly." After putting his bag by the door, Daniel came back to run a finger lightly down her cheek. "Now, where was I?"

"Telling me how Simon managed to fill his nights. I suppose he kept busy in the daytime hiring fake geologists for the reports he needed."

"They weren't fakes—just men too anxious for a payoff."

"And after all that, Simon got Edwin for the explosions?"

"To speed up the action and bring the safety factors of the mine to attention. The owners hired me then—as a last gasp," he said with a grin.

"And what a surprise Simon got!" Rosemary said in a smug tone as she leaned back against the headboard of the bed to look up at him. "I suppose he was responsible for the tire slashing and hiring 'whoever-it-was' with the pipe?"

"It will take some more doing to find out, but the police are convinced he'll finally admit it. There's plea bargaining in this part of the world, too."

"And to think he actually thought that I'd run away with him," Rosemary shuddered. "The man was mad."

Daniel sat down on the edge of the bed beside her. "He certainly was. I had no intention of ever letting you get very far from me."

She pushed upright indignantly. "But you arranged to send me to London."

"Because I wanted you out of harm's way." He pulled her close, easing her head onto his shoulder.

"I've been terrified that something would happen to you before the mine problem could be resolved."

Rosemary nuzzled into his shirt front, delighting in the clean, starched fragrance. "I wasn't much help. You *did* warn me about Simon. I hoped you were a little bit jealous," she confessed.

"More than a little bit. I wanted to knock his head off. But I didn't dare let him know that we suspected him."

"I should have known. He was carrying some dynamite caps in his briefcase the night we met, only they didn't mean anything to me. Not until I connected them with those in the box."

"Forget it. That's what I'm going to do," Daniel said, giving her a reassuring squeeze as he got up and pulled her to her feet. "We have a wedding to plan."

"You come back here," she said, clutching at his arm when he would have started for the door. "I think you've skipped one or two vital things."

His eyes crinkled with laughter as he turned and folded her against him. "No, I haven't, dearest. Not the really vital ones. They haven't been in doubt since the first time I saw you. It only took about five minutes after I tossed you out of my bedroom that first night before I was figuring on a way to get you back in—permanently. Not that you came as a total surprise," he admitted ruefully. "That partner of mine said he was sending something special my way. But even with that advance buildup, I didn't know that you were going to have such an effect on me."

"If I remember rightly, *I* was the one who was left reeling—in the annex," she said, trying to sound severe but failing completely, because his hands were on a tantalizing quest that had her body arching against him.

His voice was deep as he said, "And I was left taking a cold shower. I've had more than my share of them lately, especially after sharing that bed with you."

"I know," her gaze was suddenly shy. "I wasn't happy about your leaving it. Which is a shameless thing to admit," she added reflectively.

"Not really, we both knew what was happening to us. That's why I'm getting out of here now. No more adjoining bedrooms or anything else until there's a ring on your finger. I want everything about our love to be sane and decent and right from now on. Nothing sleazy about it," he added, casting a wry glance at the pink satin bedspread behind them. "If that's okay with you?"

She ran a wondering finger down his face, outlining his lips with a gentle touch. "Anything's all right with me. As long as you're around. You should know that, my love."

"You'll have a hard time getting rid of me for the next fifty years or so." He dropped a quick kiss on the top of her head. "Let's make tracks to London and find out how to get married in this country."

Then, as if he couldn't resist her temptation any longer, he groaned and caught her to him in a kiss that had her melting against him—unaware of anything except that she didn't ever want him to take his mouth from hers.

He was breathing raggedly when he finally lifted his head. Seeing Rosemary's ecstatic expression, he grinned again and nipped her ear. "See what I mean," he warned. "Much more of that and we'd be here until they deliver that damned early morning tea."

She squeezed his arm as they went toward the door. "What's wrong with early morning tea?"

"There's not a thing wrong with it, darling," he explained carefully, as he led her out into the hall. "I just have some other things planned for our mornings. And our afternoons. And our evenings."

"And anything in between." She smiled up at him provocatively. "Lead on, my love. I can't wait to get started."

About the Author

Glenna Finley is a native of Washington State. She earned her degree from Stanford University in Russian Studies and in Speech and Dramatic Arts, with emphasis on radio.

After a stint in radio and publicity work in Seattle, she went to New York City to work for NBC as a producer in its international division. In addition, she worked with the "March of Time" and *Life* magaine.

As a producer, she had her own show about activities in Manhattan, a show that was broadcast to England. The programs were similar to those of the "Voice of America."

Though her life in New York was exciting, she eventually returned to the Northwest where she married. Currently residing in Seattle with her husband, Donald Witte, and their son, she loves to travel, and draws heavily on her travels and experiences for the novels that have been published. Her books for NAL have sold millions of copies.